WEDDING AT SUNDAY CREEK

BY
LEAH MARTYN

MILLS
BOON

First published in Great Britain 2014
by Mills & Boon, an imprint of Harlequin (UK) Limited,
Large Print edition 2014
Eton House, 18-24 Paradise Road,
Richmond, Surrey, TW9 1SR

© 2014 Leah Martyn

ISBN: 978-0-263-23919-5

Harlequin (UK) Limited's policy is to use papers that are natural, renewable and recyclable products and made from wood grown in sustainable forests. The logging and manufacturing processes conform to the legal environmental regulations of the country of origin.

Printed and bound in Great Britain
by CPI Antony Rowe, Chippenham, Wiltshire

Dedication

For Claire, for professional insight and delicious bubbly as we celebrate the launch of my *twentieth* book for Mills & Boon.

CHAPTER ONE

DR JACK CASSIDY, trauma surgeon, part-time explorer sometimes lover, stood away from the aeroplane, slowly absorbing the rich, bold colours of the Australian outback. And thought, unlike England, there was no elegant restraint out here. The colours were in-your-face heart-stopping and glorious.

He breathed in deeply, his eyes picking out the silhouettes of a family of kangaroos grazing in a nearby paddock. Big reds, he decided, feeling exhilarated by the sight. It felt good to be *home*. Added to that, he'd finally stepped away from the train wreck of a long-term relationship and felt freer than he had in months. Riding the upbeat feeling, he wheeled back towards the plane, where his luggage was waiting on the airstrip, and bent to pick up his bags.

The hospital was only a short walk away. He

understood from his telephone interview that presently there was only one doctor at the Sunday Creek hospital, Dr Darcie Drummond. And that's where his knowledge of her began and ended. He just hoped Dr Drummond wasn't into role demarcation in the practice. If she expected him to just sit in his office and *administrate*, then she'd have to change her thinking.

Jack Cassidy intended to be a hands-on boss.

With the merest glance at her watch, Darcie decided it was time to go home. The hospital would call her if she was needed. Rolling her chair away from the desk, she stood and moved across to the window, looking out.

It was still hazy towards the west and she knew the grey bank of cloud in the sky was caused by intermittent bush fires. Nothing to worry about, the locals had assured her. It was the regular burning off of long grass or bush-fire fuel and the rural fire brigade would have everything under control.

Darcie just hoped they did…

'Knock, knock.'

She spun round, several fronds of dark hair zipping across her cheekbones as her gaze swivelled to the open doorway. A man, easily six feet if she was any judge, and someone she didn't recognise, lounged against the doorframe.

Out of nowhere, every nerve in her body jumped to attention. Darcie blinked, registering blue eyes, dark hair, knife-edge cheekbones and a mouth that had her instantly imagining fantasies that only existed in her dreams. She swallowed dryly. 'Can I help you?'

'I sure hope so.' He gave a cool imitation of a smile. 'I'm your new medical director.'

He had to be kidding.

Darcie's disbelieving gaze ran over him. She wouldn't have expected a suit and tie but this guy looked as though he'd just come down from a Himalayan trek. He was wearing combat trousers and a black T-shirt, his feet enclosed in hiker's boots that came up over his ankles.

He didn't look like a senior doctor at all.

At least, not the ones she was used to.

'I came on the plane,' he enlightened her. 'You weren't expecting me?'

'No—I mean, yes. That is, we knew you were coming, we just didn't know when.'

He rumbled an admonishing *tsk*. 'Don't you read your emails? I sent my arrival details through a couple of days ago.'

Oh, help. This was going to sound totally lame. 'Our computer's anti-virus protection has turned a bit iffy lately. It's culling messages that should be coming through to the inbox. And a tree fell over some cables yesterday, bringing the internet down. We do the best we can...'

Jack caught her cut-glass English accent and frowned a bit. What kind of a hospital was she running here? Or *attempting* to run. Switching his gaze from her heated face to the sign on her door, he queried, 'You *are* Dr Darcie Drummond?'

Almost defensively, Darcie pulled back from the intensity of his gaze and cursed the zing of awareness that sizzled up her backbone. How totally inappropriate, she admonished herself. And grief! She'd forgotten his name! 'Yes, I'm Darcie Drummond.' Moving quickly from the window, she offered her hand.

'Jack Cassidy.' He took her hand, easily enfolding it within his own.

Darcie took her hand back, almost shocked at the warmth that travelled up her arm. 'You must think this is all terribly unprofessional,' she apologised.

One eyebrow quirked above Jack Cassidy's extraordinarily blue eyes. 'Thought of getting someone in to check your computer?'

Of course they had. 'We're rather isolated here,' she said thinly, as if that should explain everything. 'Technical help is never easy. You just have to wait until they get to you.'

He made a click of annoyance. 'The hospital should have priority. You should be out there, kicking butt.'

Darcie bristled. She knew whose butt she'd *like* to kick! And she was puzzled as well. She'd read Jack Cassidy's CV. That information *had* actually come through on her email. He'd been working in London for the past year. Surely he hadn't drifted so far from his Australian roots not to realise their rural hospitals were chronically under-resourced?

'I take it you do have running water?'

Darcie's hackles rose and refused to be tamped down.

OK—he was taking the mick. She got that. But enough was enough. 'We draw water from the well outside,' she deadpanned.

Jack's smile unfolded lazily, his eyes crinkling at the corners. *Nice one, Dr Drummond.* He felt his pulse tick over. The lady had spirit. And she was a real looker. Working with her should prove…interesting.

He lowered himself onto the corner of her desk. 'I need to make a couple of phone calls, check in with the hospital board. Landline working OK?'

She sent him a cool look. 'Yes, it is.' She indicated the phone on her desk. 'Make your calls and then we'll see about getting you settled in.' With that, she turned and fled to the nurses' station.

And female solidarity.

Darcie palmed open the swing door and went through to the desk. 'He's here!'

Nurse manager Maggie Neville and RN Lauren Walker paused in mid-handover and looked up.

'Who?' Maggie queried.

Darcie hissed out the breath she'd been holding. 'The new MD.'

'Cassidy?' Maggie's voice rose a fraction. 'I didn't see anyone come through here.'

'He must have cut through the paddock and come in the back way,' Darcie said. 'He's in my office, now.'

'Oh, my stars!' Lauren's eyebrows disappeared into her blonde fringe. 'It must have been him I passed in the corridor. Big guy in combats, flinty eyes, *out there* sexy?'

Darcie nodded, her teeth meshing against her bottom lip. Lauren's description was OTT but Darcie supposed Jack Cassidy had come across as very…masculine.

Lauren snickered. 'I thought he must have been an actor come in for some treatment!'

Darcie and Maggie looked blank until Maggie asked, 'Why on earth would you think that?'

'Keep up, guys!' Lauren said, making a 'duh'

face. 'There's a reality series being shot out at Pelican Springs station. The film crew and cast are living in a kind of tent city. I can't believe you didn't know.'

'All news to me,' Maggie said cryptically. She flicked a hand. 'With you in a minute, Darc. We're just finishing up the report.' Maggie went on to tell Lauren, 'Keep an eye on Trevor Banda, please. If that old coot is up and walking—'

'I'll threaten him with a cold shower,' Lauren promised cheerfully. She slid off the high stool. '*Ciao*, then. Have a nice weekend, Maggie.'

'Chance would be a fine thing,' Maggie muttered, before returning her attention to Darcie. 'So, we have a new boss at last. Someone to take the flak. What's he like?'

Absurdly good looking. Darcie gave a one-shouldered shrug. 'He seemed a bit…*strutty*.'

'You mean stroppy?'

'No…' Darcie sought to explain. 'Strutting his authority.'

'Throwing his weight around,' Maggie interpreted with a little huff. 'Well, we'll soon sort him out.'

'Maybe it's just me,' Darcie reconsidered, thinking she had possibly said more than she should about their new boss. 'He caught me unawares. I looked up and he was just…there.'

Maggie's look was as old as time. 'Six feet plus of sex on legs, was it? That's if we can believe Lauren.'

Darcie rolled her eyes and gave a shortened version of the missing email containing Jack Cassidy's arrival details. 'He didn't seem too impressed with us,' she added bluntly.

Maggie made a soft expletive. 'Don't you dare wear any of that rubbish, Darcie. You've been here. Done the hard yards when no other doctor would come outback. And how challenging was that for someone straight out of England!'

Darcie felt guilt a mile wide engulf her. Coming to work here had had nothing to do with altruism, or challenge. It had been expediency in its rawest form that had brought her to Sunday Creek.

She'd more or less picked a place on the map,

somewhere Aaron, the man she'd been within days of marrying, would never find her. She knew him well enough to know he'd *never* connect her with working in the Australian outback.

It was that certainty that helped her sleep at night.

'I couldn't have managed any of it without you and the rest of the nurses,' Darcie apportioned fairly.

'That's why we make a good team,' Maggie asserted, picking up her bag and rummaging for her keys. 'I can hang about for a bit if you'd like me to,' she offered.

'No, Maggie, but thanks.' Darcie waved the other's offer away. 'Go home to your boys.' Maggie was the sole parent of two adolescent sons and spent her time juggling work, home and family. In the time Darcie had been here, she and Maggie had become friends and confidantes.

Although it was usually Maggie who confided and she who listened, Darcie had to admit. Somehow she couldn't slip into the confidences other women seemed to share as easily as the name of their hairdresser. 'I'll be fine,' she said now. 'And it'll be good to have a senior doctor about the place,' she added with a bravado she was far from feeling.

Jack was just putting the phone down when Darcie arrived back in her office. 'All squared away?' she asked, flicking him a hardly-there smile.

'Thanks.' He uncurled to his feet.

Taking a cursory look around her office, she moved to close one of the blinds.

'So, what are the living arrangements here?' Jack asked.

'The house for the MD is being refurbished at present, so you'll have to bunk in with the rest of us in the communal residence for now. At the moment, there's just me and one of the nurses.'

'That doesn't seem like a hardship,' he said, giving a slow smile and a nod of satisfaction.

Darcie felt nerves criss-cross in her stomach, resolving to have a word with the decorators and ask them to get a wriggle on. The sooner

Cassidy was in a place of his own where he could strut his alpha maleness to his heart's content, the better. 'The flying doctors stay over sometimes too,' she added, making it sound like some kind of buffer. 'And now and again we have students from overseas who just want to observe how we administer medicine in the outback.'

He nodded, taking the information on board.

Darcie's gaze flew over him. She'd waited so long for another doctor. Now Jack Cassidy's arrival, the unexpectedness of it, seemed almost surreal. 'Do you have luggage?'

'There didn't seem anyone about so I stashed it in what looked like a utility room on the way through.'

'We've a small team of permanent nurses who are the backbone of the place.' Darcie willed a businesslike tone into her voice. 'Ancillary staff come and go a bit.'

He sent her a brooding look. 'So, it's you and the nurses most of the time, then?'

She nodded. 'The flying doctors are invaluable, of course.'

'Whoops—sorry.' Lauren jerked to a stop in the doorway.

'Lauren.' Darcie managed a brief smile. 'This is Dr Cassidy, our new MD.'

'Jack.' He held out his hand.

'Oh, hi.' Lauren was all smiles. 'You arrived on the plane and there was no one to meet you,' she lamented.

'There was a mix-up with emails,' Darcie interrupted shortly, fed up with the whole fiasco. 'Did you need me for something, Lauren?'

'Oh, yes. I wondered if you'd mind having a word with young Mitchell Anderson.'

A frown touched Darcie's forehead. 'I've signed his release. He's going home tomorrow. What seems to be the problem?'

'Oh, nothing about his physical care,' Lauren hastily amended. 'But he seems a bit…out of sorts for someone who's going home tomorrow.'

'I'll look in on him.' Darcie sent out a contained little smile.

'Thanks.' Lauren gave a little eye flutter aimed mostly at Jack. 'I'm heading back to the station. Yell if you need me.'

'What was your patient admitted for?' Jack asked, standing aside for Darcie to precede him out of the office.

'Snakebite.'

'You know, he may just need to talk the experience through.'

Darcie shrugged. 'I'm aware of that. I tried to find a bit of common ground and initiate a discussion about snakes and their habits. I knew Mitch would be able to tell me more than I could possibly know but he didn't respond. I'd actually never seen a case of snakebite,' she admitted candidly. 'But I know the drill now. Compression, head for the nearest hospital and hope like mad they have antivenin on hand.'

'Mmm.' A dry smile nipped Jack's mouth. 'Much more civilised than in the old days. They used to pack the bite puncture with gunpowder and light the fuse. You can imagine what that did to the affected part of the body,' he elaborated ghoulishly.

If he was hoping for her shocked reaction, he wasn't going to get it. 'Pretty drastic,' she said calmly. 'I read about it in the local history section of the library.'

Jack flashed a white grin. Oh, she'd do, this one. Clever, cool and disarmingly sure of her ground as well.

It was a real turn-on.

Uh-oh. Mentally, he dived for cover. He'd just untangled his emotions from one relationship. He'd have to be insane to go looking for a replacement so quickly. But as they began to walk along the corridor towards the wards, the flower-fresh drift of her shampoo awakened his senses with a swift stab of want as incisive and sharp as the first cut of a scalpel.

CHAPTER TWO

JACK YANKED HIS thoughts up short with a barely discernible shake of his head. He needed to get back into professional mode and quickly. 'Give me the background on your patient.'

'Mitchell is sixteen.' Darcie spun her head to look at him and found herself staring into his eyes. They had the luminosity of an early morning seascape, she thought fancifully. She cleared her throat. 'He works on his parents' property about a hundred kilometres out. He was bitten on Monday last.'

'So he's been hospitalised all this week?'

'It seemed the best and safest option. I'm still getting my head around the distances folk have to travel out here. If I'd released him too early and he'd had a relapse and had to come back in—'

'So you erred on the side of caution. I'd have done the same. Where was he bitten?'

'On the calf muscle. Fortunately, he was near enough to the homestead to be found fairly quickly and he didn't panic. His parents were able to bring him straight in to the hospital.'

'You don't think he could possibly be suffering from some kind of PTSD?'

Darcie looked sceptical. 'That's a bit improbable, isn't it?'

'It can happen as a result of dog bites and shark attacks. How's he been sleeping?'

'Not all that well, actually. But I put it down to the strangeness of being in hospital for the first time.'

'Well, that's probably true. But there could be another reason why he's clammed up.' Jack's lips tweaked to a one-cornered grin. 'He's sixteen, Darcie. His testosterone has to be all over the place.'

Darcie's chin came up defensively. Same old sexist rubbish. 'Are you saying he's embarrassed around a female doctor? I was totally professional.'

'I'm sure you were.'

She swept a strand of hair behind her ear in agitation. 'Perhaps I should try talking to him again.'

'Why don't you let me?'

'You?'

'I'm on staff now,' he reminded her. 'And your Mitchell may just open up to another male. That's if you're agreeable?'

Darcie felt put on the spot. He'd given her the choice and she didn't want to be offside with him and appear pedantic. And he was, after all, the senior doctor here. 'Fine. Let's do it.'

Jack gave a nod of approval. 'Here's how we'll handle it, then.'

Mitchell was the only patient in the three-bed unit. Clad in sleep shorts and T-shirt, he was obviously bored, his gaze only intermittently on the television screen in front of him.

Following Jack's advice, Darcie went forward. 'Hi, there, Mitchell.' Her greeting was low-key and cheerful. 'Just doing a final round.'

Colour stained the youth's face and he kept his gaze determinedly on the TV screen.

'This is Dr Cassidy.' Darcie whipped the blood-pressure cuff around the boy's arm and began to pump. 'He's going to be spending some time with us here in Sunday Creek.'

'Dr Drummond tells me you crash-tackled a snake recently, Mitch.' Casually, Jack parked himself on the end of the youngster's bed. 'What kind was it?'

The boy looked up sharply. 'A western brown. They're deadly.'

'They're different from an ordinary brown, then?'

Almost holding her breath, Darcie watched her young patient make faltering eye contact with Jack. 'The western is more highly coloured.'

Jack flicked a questioning hand. 'How's that?'

'These guys aren't brown at all,' Mitchell said knowledgeably. 'They're black with a really pale head and neck. They're evil-looking. The guy that got me was about a metre and a half long.'

'Hell's teeth…' Jack grimaced. 'That's about five feet.'

'Yeah, probably. I almost peed in my pants.'

'Well, lucky you didn't do that.' Jack's grin was slow and filled with male bonding. 'I heard you kept your cool pretty well.'

Mitch lifted a shoulder dismissively. 'Out here, you have to learn to take care of yourself from when you're a kid. Otherwise you're dead meat.'

Over their young patient's head, the doctors exchanged a guarded look. This response was just what they'd hoped for. And it seemed that once started, Mitch couldn't stop. Aided by Jack's subtle prompting, he relaxed like a coiled spring unwinding as he continued to regale them with what had happened.

Finally Jack flicked a glance at his watch. 'So, it's home tomorrow?'

'Yeah.' Mitch's smile flashed briefly.

'What time are your parents coming, Mitchell?' Darcie clipped the medical chart back on the end of the bed.

'About ten. Uh—thanks for looking after me.'

He rushed the words out, his gaze catching Darcie's for the briefest second before he dipped his head in embarrassment.

'You're welcome, Mitch.' Darcie sent him a warm smile. 'And better wear long trousers out in the paddocks from now on, hmm?'

'And don't go hassling any more snakes,' Jack joked, pulling himself unhurriedly upright. 'Stay cool, champ.' He butted the kid's fist with his own.

'No worries, Doc. See ya.'

'You bet.' Jack raised a one-fingered salute.

'Thanks,' Darcie said when they were out in corridor. 'You were right,' she added magnanimously.

'It's what's called getting a second opinion,' Jack deflected quietly. 'I imagine they're a bit thin on the ground out here.'

'Awful to think I could have sent him home still all screwed up.'

'Let it go now.' Jack's tone was softly insistent. 'You've done a fine job. Physically, your patient is well again. He's young and resilient.

He'd have sorted himself out—probably talked to his dad or a mate.'

She gave an off-centre smile. 'And we can't second-guess everything we do in medicine, can we?'

'Hell, no!' Jack pretended to shudder. 'If we did that, we'd all be barking mad. Now, do you need to check on any more patients?'

She shook her head. 'I'm only next door anyway if there's a problem.'

'Good.' In a faintly weary gesture he lifted his hands, running his fingers around his eye sockets and down over the roughness of new beard along his jaw. 'So, we can call it a day, then? I need a shower, a shave and a cold beer, in that order.'

'Oh, of course. I should have realised...' Darcie forced herself to take a dispassionate look at him. There was no mistaking the faint shadows beneath his eyes.

A sliver of raw awareness startled her. The fact that suddenly she wanted to reach up and smooth away those shadows, slowly and gently, startled her even more. Especially when she reminded herself that, for lots of reasons, her trust in men was still borderline.

The staff residence was next door to the hospital with a vacant block in between. Like the hospital, it was of weathered timber with wide verandas positioned to catch the morning sun and to offer shade during the hot summers.

'Here we are.' Darcie opened the gate and they went in, the heady scent of jasmine following them up the front path.

'Hello, who's this?' Jack asked, as a blue heeler cattle dog roused himself from under the steps and slowly came to meet them.

Darcie dimpled a smile. 'That's Capone.'

'Because…?' Jack bent and stroked the dog between his ears.

'He seems to get away with everything.'

Jack chuckled. 'Is that so, chum?' The dog's black button eyes looked back innocently. 'He's quite old, then?' Jack had seen the sprinkling of white hair mottling the dog's blue-grey coat. He went on stroking. 'What's his story?'

'Apparently, he belonged to one of the old-timers of the district.' Darcie recounted the information as she'd heard it. 'He died here at the hospital and his dog wouldn't leave, wouldn't eat and just hung around.'

'So the staff adopted him?'

'Something like that. Naturally, he couldn't be kept at the hospital so gradually they coaxed him over here and he's seems content enough to stay.'

'You're a great old boy, aren't you?' Jack gave a couple of hollow thumps to the bony ridge of the dog's shoulders. He was a sucker for cattle dogs. They'd had some beauties on the farm when he'd been growing up.

'Well, he seems to have taken to you.'

'Seems to.' Jack's expression softened for a moment.

Darcie took a shallow breath, all her nerve ends twanging. What a very compelling picture they made—a big man and his dog… She beat back the sudden urge to reach for her phone and take a picture. How absurd. How sentimental. Shooting her sensible thoughts back in place, she said briskly, 'Let's go in, shall we?

'There are six bedrooms, all quite large,' Darcie said as they made their along the wide hallway. 'Our funding allows for some domestic help. Meg McLeish keeps everything ticking over. She's a real gem.'

Jack managed a polite, 'Mmm.' He didn't need this kind of detail but it was a female thing. He got that.

'You should be comfortable in here.' Darcie opened the door on the freshness of lemon-scented furniture polish.

Jack's gaze tracked over the room, taking in the king-sized bed, fitted wardrobes and bedside tables. 'This is great, Darcie. Thanks. I'll manage from here.'

Darcie took a step back. Was he was trying to get rid of her? Tough. She hadn't finished. 'There's a linen cupboard at the end of the hall where you'll find sheets and towels. Sorry there's no en suite bathroom. I think the place was built long before they were in vogue. But there are two bathrooms for communal use.'

Jack plonked himself on the edge of the bed.

'Darcie—' he held down the thread of impatience '—it's all fine, thank you.'

'OK…' Her teeth bit softly into her bottom lip. 'I'll leave you to it, then.'

He looked up sharply with a frown. Had he offended her somehow? She'd tilted her chin in a gesture he was beginning to recognise. He pulled himself upright again. 'I'll just get cleaned up.' His mouth tweaked into a wry grin. 'I promise I'll be more sociable then.'

'Fine.' Darcie spread her hands in quick acceptance and began backing away. 'Come out to the kitchen when you're through and I'll find you that cold beer.'

Barely twenty minutes later Jack joined Darcie in the kitchen. She turned from the window. 'You were quick.' Her eyes flicked over him. Cleaned up and dressed in jeans and a pinstriped cotton shirt, he looked…well, more like a senior doctor should look, she concluded a bit primly. Crossing to the fridge, she took out a beer from a six-pack and handed it to him. 'You

Aussies seem a bit territorial about your brands. I hope you like this one.'

Jack barely noticed the label and twisting open the top he took a long pull. 'Right at this moment I'd settle for any brand as long as it was cold.' He hooked out a chair. 'Are you joining me?'

She gave a stilted smile. 'I have a glass of wine here.'

'What do we do about meals?' Jack indicated she should sit at the table with him.

'At the moment there's just Lauren and me.' Darcie met his questioning look neutrally. 'So it's all been a bit haphazard, depending what shifts she's on. We tend to just grab something from the hospital kitchen. But now you're here, perhaps we should get a better system going. Do a regular shop.'

'Sounds good to me.' He rolled back his shoulders and stretched. 'What about right now? I'm starved. What can the fridge yield up?'

'There's some watermelon and fudge,' Darcie deadpanned.

'OK,' Jack said with studied calm. 'I see you've covered all the essential food groups.'

Her spontaneous laugh rippled out, the action bringing her whole face into vivid life.

Instinctively, Jack swayed forward, staring at the sweet curve of her laughing mouth. And feeling something else. *Oh, good grief.* Instantly, he took control of his wild thoughts, anchoring his feet more firmly under the table.

Darcie tilted her head to one side. 'If we'd known you were coming—'

'You'd have baked a cake,' Jack rejoined, sitting up straighter.

'Or cooked a roast.'

He chuckled. 'So, you're telling me there's nothing in the fridge we can make a meal with. No leftovers?'

She shook her head.

'A remnant of cheese? A couple of lonely eggs?'

'Sorry.'

'What about the pub, then? Food OK?'

'Pretty good. And it's steak night, if that's what you want to hear.'

'Excellent.' He downed the last of the beer and

got to his feet. 'Let's go, then, Dr Drummond. I'm shouting dinner.'

'We'll take my vehicle,' Darcie said. 'It's a bit of a step up to the town centre.'

'What do I do about getting a vehicle?' Jack asked as they walked over to her car.

'The local Rotary Club bought a new Land Rover for the MD's use. It's presently garaged at the hospital. OK if we sort all that tomorrow?'

'Yup.' Jack opened the car door, sat down and leaned back against the headrest, deciding any further conversation about the practice could wait.

It was a typical country pub, Jack observed, with a bar, a billiard table and a scattering of tables and chairs.

'There's a beer garden through there.' Darcie indicated the softly lit outdoor area. 'We just have to order at the bar first.'

'So, what would you like to eat?' He guided her to the blackboard menu. 'Uh—big choice, I see,' he said dryly. 'Steak and vegetables or steak and chips and salad.'

'I'll have the steak and salad,' Darcie said. 'No chips.'

'You don't like chips?' Jack pretended outrage.

'I like chips,' she responded, 'just not with everything.'

They ordered and were told there might be a bit of a wait. 'Let's have a drink, then,' Jack said. 'Another wine?'

She shook her head. 'Mineral water, I think.'

'OK. Me as well. I don't want to fall asleep.'

Darcie sent him a cool look. Nice to know he found her conversation so scintillating. Being Friday evening, the beer garden was crowded. 'Most folk are friendly here,' she said, returning greetings from several of the locals.

'And you've made friends since you've been here?' Jack asked as they made their way to a vacant table.

'It's been good,' she evaded lightly. 'You're getting well looked over,' she added, taking the chair he held for her.

'I'd better behave myself, then.'

'Will that be difficult?'

'I'm not given to dancing on tables, if that's what you're worried about.'

Darcie propped her chin on her upturned hand. 'I've never actually seen anyone do that.'

'I tried it once.'

'Were you drunk?'

'Are you shocked?' Jack's teasing smile warmed the space between them. 'Final interviews were over and I knew they'd offer me a place on the surgical training programme.'

She raised an eyebrow. Oh, to have such confidence. But, then, she reasoned, Jack Cassidy seemed to be brimming with it. She took a deep breath and decided to find out more about this man who had literally dropped out of the sky and was now to all intents and purposes her boss. 'So—where have you come from today?'

His mouth tipped at the corner. 'You mean by the way I was dressed?'

And his tan. 'Well, I didn't imagine you'd just arrived from London.'

'No.' He picked up his glass unhurriedly and took a mouthful of his drink. 'I've been trekking in New Guinea for the past couple of weeks. I did part of the Kokoda track. I always promised my grandfather I'd walk it for him one day. His battalion was stationed there in the Second World War.'

'So, it has some significance for Australians, then?'

He nodded. 'Our lads were heroes in all kinds of ways. I got some good pics of the general area and managed to run off some film footage too. Next time I see Pa, he'll be able to see how it is now, although it's many years on, of course.'

Darcie felt her heartbeat quicken. She guessed this was her opportunity to extend their personal relationship a little further, ask about his family. But somehow it all felt a bit…intimate. And he'd probably feel compelled to reciprocate, enquire about her family. And as yet she hadn't been able to go there in any depth— not even with Maggie. While she was still cobbling her thoughts together, her attention was distracted by the sight of one of the hotel staff making his way swiftly between tables, almost running towards them. Darcie jumped to her feet.

'What's wrong?' Jack's head spun round, his eyes following her gaze. He sensed an emergency and shoved his chair back as he stood. 'Do you know him?'

Darcie's eyes lit with concern. 'It's Warren Rowe. He's the manager—'

'Thank God you're here, Darcie.' Warren looked pale and shaken. 'The chef—young Nathan—he's had an electric shock. We need a doctor.'

'You've got two!' Jack turned urgently to Darcie. 'Grab your bag! I'll do what I can for the casualty.'

'How long has he been down?' Jack rapped out the question as the two men sped along the veranda to the kitchen.

'Not sure. Couple of minutes at most.' Warren palmed open the swing doors and jerked to a stop. He swallowed convulsively. 'It was the electric knife—'

Jack's breath hissed through his clenched teeth and in a few strides he was at the chef's side. The young man was glassily pale, blue around the lips and, worse, he was still gripping the electric knife that had obviously short-circuited and thrown him to the floor.

'I used an insulator and switched off the current at the power point,' Warren said helpfully. 'What do you need?'

'What emergency equipment do you have?' Jack had already kicked the knife away and begun CPR.

'Defibrillator and oxygen.'

'Grab them. We'll need both.'

'Oh, my God—Nathan!' Darcie burst in, her horrified look going to the young man on the floor. Dropping beside Jack, she shot open her medical case. 'Any response?'

'Not yet. Run the oxygen, please, Darcie. I need to get an airway in.'

'I can do CPR.' Warren dived in to help.

'Defib's charging.' Darcie watched as Jack positioned the tube carefully and attached it to the oxygen.

'Breathe,' he grated. 'Come on, sunshine. You can do it!'

Darcie bit her lips together. With sickening dread she waited for some movement from Nathan's chest. Waited. And watched as Jack checked for a pulse. Again and again. The nerves in Darcie's stomach tightened. 'Shocking?'

'Only option,' Jack said tersely. 'Everyone clear, please.'

Nathan's young, fit body jerked and fell. Darcie felt for a pulse and shook her head.

'Dammit! Shocking again. Clear, please.' Jack's controlled direction seemed to echo round the big old-fashioned kitchen.

Come on, Nathan. Come on! Darcie willed silently. And then…a faint jiggle that got stronger. 'We have output,' she confirmed, husky relief in her voice.

Jack's expression cleared. 'Good work. Now, let's get some fluids into this guy.' He looked up sharply. 'Has someone called an ambulance?'

'We're here, Doc.' Two paramedics stepped through with a stretcher.

Darcie looked up from inserting the cannula to receive the drip. 'Say hello to Dr Jack Cassidy, guys.' Relief was zinging through her and she gave rein to a muted smile. 'He's the new boss at the hospital—only been here a few hours.'

'And already saved a life, by the look of it. Zach Bayliss.' The senior paramedic held out his hand. 'My partner, Brett Carew.'

A flurry of handshakes ensued.

Nathan was loaded quickly. 'We'll see you across at the hospital, then, Doc?' Zach confirmed.

'We'll be over directly.' Jack turned to Warren. 'You should disconnect all power until it's been checked by the electrical authority. You might have other dodgy gear about the place.'

'Will do, Doc. Hell, I don't ever want to see a repetition of this...'

Jack looked around the kitchen. 'This will stuff up your meal preparation. Do you have a contingency plan?'

'We do. As it happens, we'd planned to put wood-fired pizzas on the menu tomorrow so we started up the brick oven for a trial run this afternoon. It's still going strong. We'll have a line of pizzas going in no time.'

Jack gave a rueful grin. 'You couldn't send a couple across to the residence, could you, mate? We still haven't have had dinner.'

'Yeah, absolutely. No worries.' Warren flicked a hand in compliance. 'On the house, of course. And thanks, Doc. Mighty job with Nathan.'

Jack waved away the thanks and they walked out together.

'Right to go, then?' Darcie had tidied up the medical debris and was waiting on the veranda.

Jack nodded and they went across to her car.

'Nathan didn't appear to have any fractures,' she said. 'But he must have landed with an almighty thump.'

'I'll check him thoroughly in Resus. Do you know if he has family to be notified?'

'Not sure. But Warren will have got onto that.'

Jack sent her a quick, narrow look. 'He said it was your initiative to have both the defib and oxygen located at the pub. Well done, Dr Drummond.'

'I was just being proactive.' Darcie shrugged

away his praise. 'There's always a crowd in the pub at the weekends. Accidents happen. The odd nasty punch-up. Even a couple of heart attacks while I've been here. Having the defibrillator and the oxygen on site seemed a no-brainer. And the staff at the pub all have first-aid knowledge.'

'Down to you as well?' Jack asked.

'And our nurse manager, Maggie Neville. You haven't met her yet.' Darcie gave a small chuckle. 'I think she could run the place if it came to it.'

'Good.' Jack stretched his legs out as far as they would go. 'Nice to have backup.'

A beat of silence.

'I was very glad to have *your* backup this evening, Jack.'

Jack felt an expectant throb in his veins. What was this? A tick of approval from the very reserved English doctor? And unless he was mistaken, her husky little compliment had come straight from her heart.

CHAPTER THREE

WHEN THEY PULLED into the hospital car park, Jack said, 'I can take over from here, Darcie. Go home. I'm sure you've more than earned a night off.'

She made a small face. 'If you're sure?'

'More than sure. I'm pulling rank, Doctor. You're officially off duty.'

'Thanks, then.' Darcie felt the weight of responsibility drop from her. 'I'd actually kill for a leisurely bath.'

'And dinner's on its way,' Jack confirmed, as he swung out of the car. 'Warren's sending over pizzas.'

Lauren stood with Jack as he made notations on Nathan's chart. 'How's he doing?' she asked quietly.

'He has entry and exit burns on his left hand

and right foot. It's obviously been a serious shock. We'll need him on a heart monitor for the next little while.'

'He's coming round.' Lauren looked down at her watch to check the young man's pulse. 'You're in hospital, Nathan,' she said as Nathan's eyes opened. 'You've had an electric shock. This is Dr Cassidy.'

'Take it easy, Nathan.' Jack was calmly reassuring. 'This contraption here is helping you breathe.'

Nathan's eyes squeezed shut and then opened.

'Pulse is fine,' Lauren reported.

'In that case, I think we can extubate.' Jack explained to their patient what he was about to do. 'You're recovering well, Nathan, and there's an excellent chance you'll be able to breathe on your own.' He turned to Lauren. 'Stand by with the oxygen, please, but let's hope he won't need it.'

Lauren noticed the surgeon's hands were gentle. Mentally, she gave him a vote of approval. In her time she'd seen extubations carried out with all the finesse of pulling nails with a claw hammer.

'I want you to cough now, Nathan,' Jack said as the tube was fully removed. 'Go for it,' he added, as Nathan looked confused. 'You won't damage anything.'

Nathan coughed obligingly.

'OK, let's have a listen to your chest now.' Jack dipped his head, his face impassive in concentration. 'Good lad.' He gave a guarded smile. 'You're breathing well.

'Thanks, Doc.' Nathan's voice was rusty. 'Guess I've been lucky. When can I get out of here?'

'Not so fast, mate.' Jack raised a staying hand. 'You've had a hell of a whack to every part of your body. We'll need to monitor you for a couple of days.'

Nathan looked anxious. 'My job—'

'Is safe,' Jack said firmly. 'Warren will be in to see you about that tomorrow. In the meantime, I want you to just rest and let the nurses take care of you.'

'And we do that very well.' Lauren gave the

young man a cheeky smile. 'Fluids as a matter of course, Doctor?'

'Please.' Jack continued writing on Nathan's chart. 'Call if there's a problem, Lauren. I'll be right over.'

'Will do. Good to have you on board, Jack,' Lauren said as they walked out.

Jack pocketed his pen and then turned to the nurse. 'What time do the shops come alive here in the mornings?'

'Depends what you need.' A small evocative smile nipped Lauren's mouth. 'There's a truckers' café that opens about five-thirty, supermarket and bakery about six, everything else around eight-thirty-ish.'

'Thanks for the heads-up.' Jack acknowledged the information with a curt nod and strode off.

'This is fantastic!' They were eating pizza straight from the box and Jack pulled out a long curl of melted cheese and began eating it with exaggerated relish. 'Why the look, Dr Drummond?' He gave a folded-in grin. 'You didn't expect us to stand on ceremony and set the table for dinner, did you?'

Darcie took her time answering, obviously enjoying her own slice of the delicious wood-fired pizza. 'I thought the present state of the fridge would have proved I'm no domestic goddess.'

'Who needs *them*?' Jack wound out another curl of cheese. 'Do you want the last piece?'

Darcie waved his offer away and got to her feet. 'I found some raspberry ripple ice cream in the freezer. Fancy some?'

Jack shook his head. 'No, thanks.'

'Cup of tea, then?'

'Any decent coffee going, by any chance?'

'There's some good instant. Near as we get can to the real stuff out here.'

'Perfect.' Jack got up from the table and moved across to the sink to wash his hands. Drying them on a length of paper towel, he moved closer to look over her shoulder as she reached up to get mugs from the top cupboard. 'Turned out all right, then, didn't it?' His voice had a gruff quality. 'Our impromptu dinner, I mean.'

He was very close and Darcie felt warning signals clang all over her body. The zig-zag of awareness startled her, unnerved her. With her breathing shallower than usual, she said, 'It was great.' She took her time, placing the mugs carefully on the countertop as though they were fine china, instead of the cheerful, chunky variety from the supermarket.

'So, Darcie...' Jack about-turned, leaning against the bench of cupboards and folding his arms. 'Do you think we'll rub along all right?'

She blinked uncertainly. In just a few hours Jack Cassidy had brought a sense of stability and authority to the place, his presence like a rock she could hang onto for dear life.

Whoa, no! Those kinds of thoughts led to a road with no signposts and she wasn't going there. The water in the electric jug came to boiling point and she switched it off. 'We'd *better* rub along,' she replied, ignoring the flare of heat in his eyes and waving light-hearted banter like a flag. 'We're the only doctors for hundreds of miles. It won't do much for morale if either of us stomps off in a hissy fit.'

Jack gave a crack of laughter. 'Do male doctors have hissy fits?'

'Of course they do! Especially in theatres.' She made the coffee quickly and handed him his mug. 'They just call it something else.'

'Thanks.' Jack met her gaze and held it. She had the most amazing eyes, he thought. They were hazel, coppery brown near the pupils, shading to dark green at the rims. And they were looking at him with a kind of vivid expectancy. 'I suppose men might have a rant,' he suggested.

'Or a tirade?'

'A meltdown?'

'Ten out of ten. That's an excellent analogy.' She smiled, holding it for a few seconds, letting it ripen on her face and then throwing in a tiny nose crinkle for good measure.

Hell. Jack felt the vibes of awareness hissing like a live wire between them. Enough to shift his newly achieved stable world off its hinges.

But only if he let it.

Lifting his coffee, he took a mouthful and winced, deciding he'd probably given his throat full-thickness burns. He had to break this proximity before he did something entirely out of character.

And kissed her.

'Uh…' His jaw worked a bit. 'Let's grab what's left of the evening and take our coffee outside to the courtyard.'

Darcie looked surprised but nevertheless picked up her mug and followed him. 'I'll just turn on the outside light,' she said. 'We don't want to break our necks in the dark.'

'There's plenty of moonlight.' Jack looked around him as they sat at the old wooden table. The smell of jasmine was in the air. It twisted around a trellis at least six feet high. 'I guess this place would have a few stories to tell,' he surmised.

'Probably.' Darcie took a careful mouthful of her coffee.

Tipping his head back Jack looked up, his gaze widening in awe at the canopy of stars, some of which looked close enough to touch, while myriad others were scattered like so much fairy dust in the swept enormous heavens. So very different from London. 'You're a long way from home, Darcie.'

Darcie tensed. She'd expected the question or something similar but not quite so soon. For a heartbeat she was tempted to lower her guard and tell him the plain, unvarnished truth. But to do that would make her feel vulnerable. And perhaps make *him* feel uncomfortable, or worse even—sorry for her. And she so did not want that from any man. 'This is Australia.' She feigned nonchalance with an accompanying little shrug. 'So I imagine I must be a long way from home. But this is *home* now.'

Jack heard the almost fierce assertiveness in her voice. OK, he wouldn't trespass. Darcie Drummond obviously had her ghosts, the same as he did. But he liked to think he'd laid his to rest. On the other hand, he had a feeling young Dr Drummond here appeared to be still running from hers.

'So, tell me a bit about Sunday Creek,' he said evenly. 'No GP here, I take it?'

'Not for a long time. Anyone with a medical problem comes to the hospital.'

'So we take each day as it comes, then?'

'Yes.' She smiled into the softness of the night. 'I've treated a few characters.'

He chuckled. 'It's the outback. Of course you have.' With subtlety, he pressed a little further, determined to get to know her better. 'Any one instance stand out?'

'Oh, yes.' She smiled, activating a tiny dimple beside her mouth. 'Pretty soon after I'd arrived here I had a call out to one of the station properties. There'd been an accident in the shearing shed. I was still at the stage of being wide-eyed with wonder at the size and scope of everything.'

'That figures.' Jack tilted his head, listening.

'When I stepped inside the shearing shed I was thrown with the hive of activity. I'm sure I must have stood there gaping, wondering where to go or whom I should speak to. Then one of the men bellowed, "Ducks on the pond!" and suddenly there was this deathly kind of silence.'

Jack's laughter rippled.

Darcie pressed a finger to her lips, covering an upside-down smile. 'You know what it means, of course?'

'Yep.' He shot her a wry half-grin. 'It's simply shorthand for, "Mind your language, there's a lady present."'

'I had to ask Maggie when I got back to the hospital,' Darcie confessed. 'But the men were very kind to me and, fortunately, the emergency was only a case of a rather deep wound that needed suturing. I stayed for morning tea in the shed. I think I managed OK,' she added modestly.

'From the sound of it, I'd say you managed brilliantly.' In the moonlight, Jack's gaze softened over her. She was gutsy and no slouch as a doctor. He already had proof of that. He wondered what her story was. And why she'd felt the need to practise her skills so far from her roots.

Leaning back in his chair, he clasped his hands behind his head. 'I'll cover the weekend. I want you to have a break.'

'Oh.' Darcie looked uncertain. 'Shouldn't I hand over officially?'

'We can do that *officially* on Monday. Meanwhile, I'll get a feel for things in general, talk to a few faces.'

'I won't know what to do with myself…' The words were out before she could stop them.

'Have some fun,' Jack suggested. 'See your friends.'

He made it sound so simple—so normal. And it would look pathetic if she hung around the house for the entire weekend. Her brain quickly sorted through the possibilities. She supposed she did have a couple of friends she could visit—Louise and Max Alderton. They lived on a property, Willow Bend, only ten miles out. Louise was on the hospital board and somehow had sensed Darcie's need for a no-strings kind of friendship.

She could give Lou a call now. She'd still be up. See if it was OK to visit. Maybe they could go for a ride… 'OK. I'll do that. Thanks.'

Next morning, Darcie couldn't believe she'd slept in. If you called seven-thirty sleeping in, she thought wryly, sitting up to look out at the new day. The sun had risen, the temperature climbing already. Blocking a yawn, she stretched and threw herself out of bed. She had a holiday.

And she'd better remember there was a man in the house. Slipping into her short dressing gown, she sprinted along the hallway to the bathroom.

As she dressed, Darcie sensed something different about the place. A feeling of the house coming alive. And there was a delicious smell of grilling bacon coming from the kitchen.

And that could mean only one thing. Jack was up and around and amazingly he must be cooking breakfast. She hoped he'd made enough for two because she intended joining him.

As she made her way along the hallway to the kitchen, her newly found confidence began faltering. Perhaps she was being presumptuous. She didn't expect Jack to feed her. She really didn't.

But already her preconceived ideas about him had begun falling like skittles. He wasn't *strutty*—just competent. And from what she'd observed, he seemed straightforward and she liked that. If he'd only made breakfast for one, then he'd tell her so.

She paused at the kitchen door, ran her tongue around the seam of her lips and said, 'You're up early.'

Busy at the cooker top, Jack turned his head and gave her a casual 'Morning. How do you like your eggs?'

'Um…' Darcie's mouth opened and closed. 'Scrambled, I think.' She joined him at the stove. He was turning sausages and the bacon was set aside in the warming oven.

'Me too.' He gave her a quick smile. 'Will you do that while I watch these guys?'

'Yes, sure.' She looked around and saw a pile of groceries had been unloaded onto the benchtop. 'Have you been to the supermarket already?'

'I was awake early,' he said. 'Thought I'd do a quick swoop. I borrowed your car. I hope that's all right?'

'Of course.' Darcie searched for a bowl and

began cracking the eggs. 'You must let Lauren and me pay for our share of the groceries.'

'We can talk about that later,' Jack dismissed. 'Tomatoes for you?'

'Yes, please.' Darcie's mouth began to water. All this home cooking was beginning to heighten her taste buds. 'And I'll make some toast. Did you get bread?'

'I did. The baker had his front door open a crack. I gave him a shout, introduced myself and he obligingly sold me a couple of loaves.'

'That'll be Jai.' Darcie found the wholemeal loaf and hacked off a couple of slices. 'He and his wife, Nikki, relocated from Thailand. He makes gorgeous bread.'

Jack piled the cooked sausages onto a plate. 'Should we keep some of this food for Lauren?'

'Uh-uh. She'll sleep for ages. And she's vegetarian anyway.'

'Oh—OK. Good for her,' Jack said, though he sounded doubtful. 'We won't have continuous tofu to look forward to, will we?'

Darcie chuckled. 'Tofu is the new meat. But

she's more a risotto person. Although she does a great grilled halloumi and courgette salad.'

'You mean zucchini? Well, that sounds all right, as long as there's a nice T-bone steak to go with it,' he said with wry humour. 'This is about ready. Should we tuck in?'

'I'll get the plates.'

'I hope it's up to scratch,' he said.

'Oh, it will be.' Darcie was adamant. 'You seem like an amazingly good cook.'

'I was reared on a cattle property,' Jack said, as they settled over their meal. 'We all had to learn to throw a meal together, especially at mustering time. If you were given kitchen duties, you had to have something ready to feed the troops or risk getting a kick up the backside. Sorry…' His mouth pulled down. 'That sounded a bit crass.'

'Not at all.' Darcie dismissed his apology. 'So, are there a lot of you in the family?'

'I'm the eldest of five. Two brothers, two sisters. I recall some pretty rowdy mealtimes.'

And he made it sound so warm and wonderful. Darcie felt the weight of her own solitary childhood sit heavily on her shoulders. Meals on your own didn't have much going for them. But that was her *old* life. She shook her head as if to clear the debris and firmly closed the lid on that particular Pandora's box. She drummed up a quick smile. 'So, happy childhood, then?'

'Mmm.' Jack hadn't missed the subtlety of her mood change or her quickly shuttered look. But he didn't want to be stepping on any of her private landmines. One thing he did know, he'd shut up about his happy childhood.

'So, what are your plans for today?' He'd already noticed her boots, jeans and soft white shirt.

'I'm going riding.' She filled him in about the Aldertons and Willow Bend. 'You'll probably meet Lou sooner rather than later. She's on the hospital board and a great innovator.'

'Excellent. As the sole MOs for the entire district, we need all the help we can get.'

They batted light conversation around for the rest of the meal.

'You'll find a set of keys for your use at the nurses' station,' Darcie said, as they finished breakfast and began clearing the table. 'Including those for your vehicle.'

'Thanks.' He bent and began stacking the dishwasher.

Darcie blinked a bit. Heavens, he really was house-trained. 'Natalie Britten will be the RN on duty and with a bit of luck a couple of our ancillary staff should turn up as well. There's a list of numbers to call if there are any staffing problems.'

'You like all your ducks in a row, don't you?'

Darcie's chin came up. 'We're running a hospital,' she countered. 'We have to make some effort for things to be orderly.'

'That wasn't my first impression.' He smiled then, a little half-smile that seemed to flicker on one side of his lips before settling into place.

'A tiny glitch.' Darcie shrugged away his comment. 'I think you enjoyed surprising us.'

'Perhaps I did.' He considered her for a long moment. 'Will you be home tonight?' Oh, good grief! He squirmed inwardly. He'd sounded like her *father*!

Darcie looked up warily. Was he enquiring whether she had a boyfriend who might be wanting to keep her out all night? Well, let him wonder about that. 'Yes, I'll be home. But I may be late.'

Jack closed the door on the dishwasher and stood against it. 'Have a good day, then.'

'I shall.' She hovered for a moment, pushing her hands into the back pockets of her jeans. 'Thanks for this, Jack. The day off, I mean.'

He shrugged. 'You're probably owed a zillion.'

'If there's an emergency…'

He sent her a dry look. 'If I need you, I'll call you. Now scoot.' He flicked his fingers in a shooing motion. 'Before I reassign you.'

She scooted.

Jack wandered out onto the veranda, the better to take in the vibe of his new surroundings. Leaning on the timber railings, he looked down at the wildly flowering red bottlebrush. The hardiest of the natives, it simply produced more and more blossoms, regardless of the vagaries of the seasons.

Raising his gaze, he looked out towards the

horizon. There was a ribbon of smoke-laden cloud along the ridge tops. So far it obviously wasn't a cause for concern. He hoped it stayed that way…

The clip of Darcie's footsteps along the veranda interrupted his train of thought. He swung round, a muscle tightening in his jaw, an instinct purely male sharpening every one of his senses. She'd gathered up her hair and tied it into a ponytail and she'd outlined her mouth with a sexy red lipstick.

His heart did a U-turn. His male antennae switched to high alert. Hell. This was right out of left field.

He fancied her.

Darcie stopped beside him, dangling her Akubra hat loosely between her fingers. 'Taking in the scenery?' Her quick smile sparkled white against the red lipstick.

'Just getting acquainted with the possibilities.' *And wasn't that the truth.*

'Good,' she said lightly, and proceeded down the steps. At the bottom she turned and looked back. 'Don't wait up.'

Cheeky monkey. Jack dipped his head to hide a burgeoning grin and countered, 'Don't fall off.'

Then, with something like wistfulness in his gaze, he watched as she reversed out of the driveway and took off.

His hands tightened their grip on the railings, some part of him wanting to rush after her, flag her down.

And spend the entire day with her.

CHAPTER FOUR

DARCIE HALF WOKE to the sound of knocking on her bedroom door. For a few seconds she struggled to open her eyes, calling groggily, 'Who is it?'

'It's Jack. Can you come to the door, please? We have an emergency.'

Jack? Jack…? Darcie closed her eyes again.

Hell, what was she doing? Jack glanced at his watch. He rapped on the door again. 'Wake up, Darcie! I need to speak to you!'

Jack! Oh, good grief! Darcie sat bolt upright as reality struck. Throwing herself out of bed, she padded over to the door. 'What time is it?' She blinked up at him.

'Five o'clock—' He stopped abruptly. She was pulling on a gown over a short ruby-red nightie, her breasts moving gently beneath the silk. *Hell.* His breath jagged in his throat. He stepped back and blinked. 'Uh—we have an emergency out where some kind of film is being shot. Do you know about it?'

'Not really. Lauren mentioned it. What's happened?'

'Apparently two of the actors have fallen into a disused well. The message the ambulance got was pretty garbled. But they've asked for medical backup. I'm sorry to disrupt your sleep-in but I think this needs both of us.'

'OK…' Darcie pushed the heavy fall of hair back from her cheek. 'Give me a few minutes.'

'I'll meet you out front. Don't mess about.'

Darcie made a face at the closing door. She pulled on jeans and T-shirt and pushing her feet into sturdy trainers she sprinted to the bathroom.

Armed with a couple of trauma kits from the hospital, they travelled in Jack's Land Rover. 'I've spoken to Mal Duffy, the police sergeant,' Jack said. 'He's given me directions to the site. It's about forty Ks.'

'So, apart from the ambulance, who's in on this jaunt?'

'The state emergency service.'

Darcie nodded. She was well acquainted with the SES and their dedicated volunteers. 'Mal heads up the local SES. Their vehicle with the rescue gear is kept at the police station but he'll have to try to get a team together. At this early hour on a Sunday, it could be difficult.'

Jack raised an eyebrow, seeming impressed with her local knowledge. 'In that case, we'll just have to wing it until they get there.'

'Why on earth would they be filming so early?' she wondered aloud.

'Maybe they wanted to catch a special effect with the light.'

She glanced at him sharply. 'You know something about making films, then?'

'Oh, yeah.' He gave a hard, discordant laugh. 'My *ex* is an actress.'

For a moment his words formed an uncomfortable silence between them. Darcie glanced at his profile but it told her nothing. Was he sad or mad or both? 'Ex-*wife*?'

'No.' He paused infinitesimally. 'We didn't get that far. We'd been together for three years. But our jobs took us in different directions. In the end, the relationship proved unworkable.'

Of course, it hadn't helped that when he'd got to England, where Zoe had been filming, she'd found someone else. He swallowed the residue of bitterness. His ego had taken a hard kick, but life moved on. And thank heaven for that.

'I guess relationships are tricky at the best of times,' Darcie responded quietly. 'Do you have any idea what size this well might be?' She changed conversation lines tactfully.

'Going by my acquaintance with wells, I'd guess six by six in the old measurements.'

'So—the size of a small room,' she said consideringly.

Jack took his eyes off the road for a second to look at her. 'Any problems with confined spaces?'

'I've done a little caving...' Darcie recognised the flutter of uncertainty in her stomach. 'I don't know how that equates with going down into a well.'

'Only one way to find out,' Jack said. 'It'll be dark inside and there'll probably be rubble at the bottom. And I mean anything from rocks to old furniture. Usually, when a well is closed, some effort is extended to part fill the hole to make it less of a hazard. We'll need to look out for rats as well.'

'Rats?' Darcie suppressed a shudder. 'I hope they're dead ones and long gone.' A frown touched her forehead. 'It's daylight pretty early these days—how come they wouldn't have known the well was there?'

'I doubt it would have been used for years, and it's possible that some attempt would have been made to cover it over.'

'Well, whatever they did hasn't been good enough. Why wouldn't they build a roof or something?'

'A roof!' Jack hooted. 'You've still a lot to learn about life in the Australian bush, Darcie. Our graziers have to make the best use of their time to stay viable. They can't go around erecting a roof over every well they close. More than likely, they would have chucked some logs across the top. But with time they'll have become overgrown, which will have only served to camouflage the rotting wood beneath.'

'And there you have an accident waiting to happen,' Darcie concluded.

'By George, she's got it!'

Darcie gave an exaggerated eye roll. 'How much further, do you think?'

'Hmm…ten Ks possibly.'

'I hate this part of being a doctor out here,' she admitted candidly. 'Flying by the seat of your pants, not knowing what you'll find when you get there.'

'Comes with the territory, Darcie. You work as an outback doctor, you take on board the highs and lows.' And if she hadn't come to a realisation of that by now, then what the hell was she doing here?

'I understand all that, Jack,' she defended. 'It's just…medically, you can only do so much. And it's so *far* from everything.'

Jack felt his mood softening. 'Granted, we don't have the backup of a casualty department,' he conceded. 'So we make adjustments. In our heads as well as practically.' After a minute, he added, 'Whatever path we follow in life, we're probably conditioned by our backgrounds.'

'Perhaps we are.'

'I found working in London stressful.'

'Did you?' She sounded surprised.

'You bet. London is an amazing city, so many centuries of history, but I felt as isolated in the heart of its busyness as you possibly do here in these great open spaces. I'm human too, Doctor. Just like you…'

They turned to each other, eyes meeting. Seeing the slow warmth in his, Darcie's heart gave a little jiggle of recognition.

Suddenly, she felt a lift in her spirits, unexpectedly buoyed by his take on things. Perhaps they had, in quite different ways, quite a lot in common.

Within minutes they were at the location.

'OK, let's get cracking,' Jack snapped, as they alighted from the Land Rover. He moved to organise the gear they'd need, tossing Darcie one of the high-visibility vests the hospital had included.

Quickly, Darcie slid into the vest and secured the fastenings. 'We'd better find out who's in charge.'

'That looks like a site office.' Jack indicated the prefab building. 'We'll enquire there.'

A short, stocky man behind the desk shot to his feet as Jack rapped and stuck his head in. 'Blake Meadows,' he said, and held out his hand. 'I'm the film unit manager.' His gaze flicked to Darcie and back to Jack. 'You're the doctors?'

'Yes.' Jack made the introductions. 'What can you tell us?'

'Two of our young actors, Jessica and Lachlan, have fallen into the well. We've managed to gather a few details. Jess caught her arm on a piece of protruding metal on the way down.'

'So there's bleeding,' Darcie surmised.

The manager nodded. 'At the moment, she's been able to staunch it with her T-shirt.'

'And the other casualty?' Jack asked.

'Lachy hasn't been so fortunate.' Blake Meadows made a grimace. 'According to Jess, he landed on something hard—rocks maybe. Passed out. It's his leg...' He rubbed a hand across his face. 'If this gets out, we'll be in the news for all the wrong reasons. The company doesn't need this.'

'I don't imagine the young people needed it either.' Jack was tight-lipped. 'Can you direct us to the well?'

'I'll take you.' The manager hurried them from the office and towards an army-type Jeep parked nearby.

'We probably won't be able to do much until the SES gets here,' Jack said, as they scrambled aboard and took off.

'They should be right behind you,' Blake said. 'Frankly, I'm staggered with the promptness of everyone's response.'

Well, at least their attendance was appreciated, Darcie thought critically, hanging on for dear life as they rocked through the scrubby terrain towards the accident site.

To their surprise, Mal Duffy was already on the scene when they arrived. He greeted both doctors. 'Knew a short cut,' he explained in his slow drawl. 'This is my team for today. Meet Rod and Gez.'

With no time to waste, Mal and his team began erecting a tripod arrangement over the top of the well.

'Do we have any head torches?' Jack queried. 'It's going to be pretty dark down there.'

'Ah—unfortunately, we don't have any in stock,' Mal apologised. 'The lantern torches are high-powered and we'll place them to give you maximum light. Best we can do.'

'Put head torches on your list of priorities, then, please,' Jack countered thinly.

'Will do, Doc. Sorry for the glitch.'

'Has the air ambulance being notified?' Jack asked.

'CareFlight chopper is on its way,' Mal said. 'There's a helipad at Pelican Springs homestead. It's only about ten Ks from here. So once we get the casualties out, our ambos can shoot them across to meet the chopper.'

Jack's mouth compressed briefly. It all sounded straightforward enough but experience had taught him it probably wouldn't be. And if that was the case, then they'd just have to deal with any curve balls as they were thrown.

Mentally, Darcie began to prepare herself, watching as the SES team made their preparations.

'You OK?' Jack asked, shooting her a sideways glance.

'Fine.' She flicked a hand toward the SES team. 'I take it we're hooked up to this pulley thing and get lowered in?'

Jack nodded. 'We'll wear a safety harness. I'll drop in first and the SES guys will retrieve the rope and send you down. OK, looks like they're ready for us.'

Within seconds, Darcie found herself swinging down into the well. She gave a little gasp as she landed unevenly on some kind of rubble. Releasing herself from the guide rope, she began to take her bearings. It was darkish in the cavity, as Jack had predicted, and the place had a repulsive odour. 'Jack?'

'Right here.'

'Oh…' Darcie nudged in beside him, watching as he aimed his torch across to the other side of the well, locating their patients. She heard the girl's subdued whimper and said quietly, 'I'll take Jessica.'

'Thanks. I'll see what's happening with Lachlan.'

Swinging the trauma pack from her shoulders, Darcie hunkered down beside the injured girl. 'Hi, Jess,' she said softly. 'I'm Darcie. I'm a doctor. Can you tell me where you're hurt?'

'It's my arm. I've been so scared…' Her teeth began chattering,

'And you're cold.' Darcie unfolded a space blanket from her supplies and tucked it around the girl. 'Did you hit your head at all?' she asked, beginning to test Jessica's neuro responses.

'No. I've done some stuntwork. I know how to fall safely. But Lachy's really hurt, I think.' She squeezed her eyes shut. 'Please…' she whispered on a sob. 'Can you get us out of here?'

Darcie felt put on her mettle. Quickly, she sifted through her options.

Both Jess's neuro responses and pulse were fine but she needed to be got out of this hell-hole and into the fresh air. 'I'll just need to check your arm, Jess.' Gently, Darcie removed the bloodstained T-shirt. She pursed her lips. Jess had a deep gash from the point of her shoulder to her mid upper arm. The site was already swelling and dark blue with bruising. It was still oozing blood. Thankfully, there was no artery involved.

OK. Mentally, Darcie squared her shoulders. She needed to show some initiative here. She took the girl's uninjured hand and held it. 'Jess, we have trained people waiting up top. I'm going to signal for one of them to come down with a retrieval harness and take you up. The paramedics will take care of you until I can get up there and assess you properly. Is that OK?'

Jessica nodded. 'My arm's throbbing…'

'I'll give you something before you go. Do you feel sick at all?'

'Bit…'

Darcie nodded. 'I'll give you something to combat the nausea as well. You've been really brave, Jess,' Darcie said, shooting home the painkiller and anti-emetic. 'Now, let's get you up and out of here.'

It was all accomplished quickly and skilfully.

With Jessica safely out, Darcie concentrated on helping Jack with their other casualty. 'How's Lachlan?'

'Fractured NOF possibly. But we can't diagnose accurately without an MRI. His belly appears soft so it's safe to get a line in.'

'I think he's coming round.' Darcie felt a rush of relief.

'It's OK, Lachlan.' Jack's manner was calmly reassuring. 'You've fallen into a well, buddy. Knocked yourself out. I'm Jack and this is Darcie. We're doctors.'

Lachlan sucked air in through his lips. 'Leg...' he groaned. 'Pain's epic...'

'Yep. Hang in there, matey.' Jack gently lifted the youngster's head and applied the oxygen mask. 'Will you draw up morphine five and maxolon ten, please, Darcie? We don't want him throwing up on us. As soon as we get him stable, we'll follow with fifty of pethidine. That should get him through transportation to the hospital.'

Darcie shot home the injections quickly.

'Let's start splinting now,' Jack said. 'The sooner we get this lad out of here the better.'

Darcie's eyes were on high alert for any changes in Lachlan's condition as she watched Jack place the supportive splints between the young man's legs. 'Bandages now?'

'Nice thick ones,' Jack confirmed.

'This shouldn't have happened, should it?' Darcie said, working swiftly to bind Lachlan's injured leg to his good one.

'Not if the location scouts were on top of their game,' Jack agreed gruffly. 'I think I'll be having a word to the Workplace Health and Safety people.'

'Report them?' Darcie felt a lick of unease.

'Just doing my job, Darcie.' Jack was unequivocal. He looked at Lachlan's still form. 'Whack him with the pethidine now, please. I'll make my way back over to the opening and give the guys a shout for the stretcher.'

As Jack moved away from her peripheral vision, Darcie felt the cave-like atmosphere close in on her, her hearing fixed on every tiny sound. A fragment of leaf-like debris floated down and landed on her shoulder. She gave an involuntary shudder, shaking it off, feeling the nerves in her stomach crawl. The conditions in the well were awful.

Darcie pulled herself up with a jerk. This wasn't the time to start losing it. She had a seriously ill patient depending on her skills as a doctor. About to draw up the drug, she stopped and froze. In a second everything had changed. Lachlan was gulping, his eyes rolling back in his head, his colour ashen.

'Jack!' Darcie's cry echoed off the earthen walls. Instinctively, she ripped open Lachlan's shirt and began chest compressions.

'What's happened?' Jack's bulk dropped beside her.

'He's arrested!'

Jack's expletive scorched the air. He would have to intubate.

With the speed of light, he began zipping open sections of the trauma pack, gathering equipment. Centring himself for a second, he prepared to carry out the emergency procedure. And drew back sharply. He cursed under his breath. This wasn't going to work. He needed more light…

But there was none. He'd have to make do, feel his way.

Slowly, slowly, he passed the tube down Lachlan's trachea, attaching it to the oxygen. 'Now, breathe for me, Lachy,' he grated. 'Come on!' He waited a second and then checked the carotid pulse in the young man's neck.

Nothing.

'We'll have to defib him.' Jack reached for the life pack. 'We are *not* losing this one, Darcie.' Jack's voice roughened. 'I'm counting on you.'

Darcie's expression was intense. Every compression meant life for Lachlan. Her heart began to pound against the walls of her chest, her pulse thumping in her wrists and throat. She began feeling light-headed, perspiration patching wetly across her forehead and in the small of her back. 'Jack, hurry…'

'This is a bloody nightmare,' Jack hissed between clenched teeth. 'Be ready to take over the bag when I defib,' he snapped.

Darcie captured a rush of strength from somewhere. Whether Lachlan ever woke again could depend on their teamwork now.

'OK—do it!' Jack's command rang out.

Almost in slow motion Darcie reached out and took over the Air-Viva bag.

'And clear!'

Darcie dropped the bag and sprang back, willing the volts of electricity to do their work and kick-start Lachlan's heart.

A beat of silence.

'Jack?'

'Nothing. Let's go to two hundred. Clear!'

Darcie strove to keep panic at bay, aware only of its grip on her gut and the slow slide of sweat between her breasts.

'Start compressions again, Darcie.' Jack looked haunted. 'I'm giving him adrenaline.'

Darcie nodded, not capable of verbalising her reply.

Jack's mouth snapped into a thin line, his fingers curling round the mini-jet, which already contained the lifesaving drug. 'Come on, baby—do your job!' he implored, sending the needle neatly between Lachlan's ribs and into his heart. 'Clear!' He activated the charge.

A breathless hush as they waited.

Into the silence, the trace began bleeping and then shot into a steady rhythm. 'Yes…' Jack's relief was subdued.

Darcie slumped forward, her energy spent. She felt the threat of tears and held the heels of her hands against her eyes, gathering her composure. 'Oh, sweet heaven…'

Jack's arm came round her shoulders. 'Hey…'

'I'm OK…'

'You're not.' Jack turned her into his arms and held her.

Darcie allowed herself to be held, feeling the warmth of his body mingle with hers, melting into him, drawing strength from his strength and…the maleness of him. A need she hadn't known existed rose in her, but before she could wonder at its completeness she felt the swift stab of reality. She drew back sharply. What on earth had she been thinking of?

Lachlan was waking up, fear and confusion clouding his eyes.

'It's OK, Lachy.' Darcie beat back her own confusion. She took his hand and squeezed. 'You'll be fine.'

Jack swallowed, clearing the lump from his throat. He felt as though an invisible punch had landed in his solar plexus. She'd felt so right in his arms. And he'd so nearly kissed her. Taken that soft, beautiful mouth with his. And kissed her. Idiot. He drew in a quick, hard breath. 'Think a shot of midazolam is called for here, Dr Drummond?'

'I'd say so.' Darcie nodded, glad for the return to professionalism. The drug would act as a light anaesthetic and ease Lachy over the trauma of the next few hours. She turned away. 'Would you do it, please, Jack?' She wrapped her arms around her midriff, feeling hollowed out.

'Nice work, guys.' Zach Bayliss loomed out of the shadow, towing the collapsible stretcher. 'Could have been a whole different story, couldn't it?'

Darcie felt as though she'd been to hell and

back. Swallowing hard on the tightness in her throat, she pulled herself upright. 'He's ready to move now, Zach. We've got him back into sinus rhythm but he'll have to be watched.'

'Understood, Doc.' Zach was a seasoned paramedic. He knew well the battle that had been fought here and, for the moment, won. 'Let's get this youngster on his way, then. If you're ready, Jack, on my count.'

In unison, they gently rolled Lachlan first on one side then the other, sliding each section of the supporting plinth under him and snapping the pieces together. A sturdy rope was attached to each end of the stretcher and almost immediately it was being winched safely to the top.

With Lachlan safely loaded into the ambulance, the emergency crew gathered around. It had already been decided Jess's care could be safely managed at Sunday Creek hospital.

'Where do you want Lachy sent, Jack?' Zach gave one last look inside the ambulance and closed the doors.

'The Royal in Brisbane is our best chance.'

Jack was already pulling out his mobile phone. 'I'll alert the head of the trauma team, Nick Cavello. He'll coordinate everything from his end.'

'CareFlight chopper's landed at Pelican Springs.' Mal Duffy joined the group.

'We'll take off, then.' Zach sketched a farewell wave. 'You're OK with Jess travelling with you and Jack, Darcie?'

'I've already settled her in the back seat,' Darcie confirmed. 'Take care of Lachy.'

'Will do.' Zach threw himself into the driver's seat of the ambulance. 'Thanks, everyone,' he called, before starting the engine. Within seconds, the emergency vehicle was being manoeuvred carefully away down the bush track.

CHAPTER FIVE

'JUST RELAX, JESS,' Darcie said, as they prepared for the trip back to Sunday Creek. 'We'll have you much more comfortable soon.'

'I'll try to minimise the bumps in the road.' Jack tried to inject some lightness into the situation and Jess gave a weak smile. 'Hang in there, kiddo,' he added gently. 'You're doing great.'

The return trip was covered mostly in silence as though each was busy with their own thoughts. As they reached the outskirts of the township, Jack said, 'It's still your day off, Darcie. I'll assume Jess's care if you like.'

'Thanks, but that's not necessary,' she answered firmly. 'Jess is my patient. I'd like to follow through.'

'Fine.' He glanced at her sharply with a frown. 'We'll need to debrief at some stage.'

Well, she knew that. Darcie rubbed at her collarbone through the thin material of her T-shirt. But if Jack had any thoughts of them *debriefing* about what had almost happened back there in the cave…

Soon they'd reached the hospital and Jack was reversing into the ambulance bay.

Dan Prentice, the hospital's only orderly, was waiting with a wheelchair and Jessica's transfer was made without fuss.

'Oh, hi, guys, you're back.' Natalie hurried forward.

'This is Jess, Nat.' Darcie kept her hand on her young patient's shoulder. 'Could you take her through to the treatment room, please? I'm just going to grab a quick shower and then I'll be back to suture Jess's arm.'

A quick shower meant just that. And years of practice meant Darcie had the logistics down pat. When she got back to the unit, Natalie had Jess ready in a gown, had drawn up lignocaine and opened the suture packs. 'Thanks, Nat. This all looks good.' Darcie gloved, pleased her patient was looking more relaxed. 'Little sting now, Jess,' she said, injecting the anaesthetic and infiltrating the wound. 'How's your tetanus status these days?'

'I had a top-up before I went on the film shoot.'

'Good.' Darcie smiled. 'That's one less jab we'll have to give you.' After several minutes she sought Jess's reaction and judged the anaesthetic had taken effect. 'Right, we're set to go. Nat, would you flush with normal saline, please? And, Jess, feel free to chill out, maybe have a little doze?'

Darcie's suturing was neat and painstakingly precise.

'You're so good at this,' Natalie murmured.

Darcie gave a half-laugh. 'I used to get hauled over the coals for being too slow.'

'I think suturing is an art,' Natalie maintained. 'In fact, everything about practising medicine is an art—at least, it should be.'

'Oh, if only that were true...'

Darcie inserted the final stitch. 'That's it.' She stripped off her gloves and stood back to enable Natalie to place a non-stick dressing over the wound. 'Jess, honey…' She roused her patient gently.

'Oh…' Jess's eyes fluttered open. She looked dazed for a second. 'Am I done?'

'Like a good roast.' Natalie chuckled. 'Dr Drummond's done a pretty fancy job with your stitches.'

'Thanks…' Jess blinked a bit. 'You've been really kind…' Two tears tracked down the youngster's cheeks and she wiped them away with the tips of her fingers.

Darcie pulled up a stool and sat down next to her patient. Poor kid. She'd been through a terrible ordeal. 'I want you put everything aside and just rest now, Jess. Think you can do that?'

Jessica bit her lip. 'I guess…'

'And I'd like to keep you here overnight.' And maybe for an extra one or two, Darcie thought. There could be residual effects from Jess's fall that would only become apparent later on. She gave her patient a reassuring smile. 'Now, can I call anyone for you—parents, perhaps?'

Jess shook her head. 'My parents live in Sydney. No need to alarm them. I'll call them when

I'm up and around again. Mum would probably come racing out here and want to do my
washing,' she added with a spark of humour.
'Where's Lachy?'

'We've sent him to Royal Brisbane. Dr Cassidy arranged that so I'm sure he'll get an up-
date on Lachy's condition later today and let
you know.' Darcie stood to her feet. 'Now, Nat
will get you settled on the ward and I'll look in
on you a bit later, all right? If you need a cer-
tificate for time off work, I'll take care of that
as well.'

'I'm not going back there.' Jess shook her head
firmly. 'They can shove their job.'

Mentally, Darcie stepped back. There was a
raft of separate issues here and after what had
happened to her, Jessica was probably not in
the right frame of mind to be making snap de-
cisions about her job. Obviously, she needed to
talk things through but that could wait. Darcie
picked up the notes. 'Your arm will probably
ache a bit after the anaesthetic wears off,' she
told her patient. 'I'll write up some pain relief
for you.'

'And don't be a martyr,' Natalie chimed in with a grin. 'Just yell if you need something.'

Jack was taking his time about things. He'd hauled the trauma packs through to the utility room, repacking them and replacing the items they'd used. They were now ready for the next emergency.

Strictly, it wasn't his responsibility, he conceded, but Sunday Creek wasn't a big city hospital and everyone had to pull their weight wherever it was needed. Even senior doctors. Besides, he admitted a bit ruefully, he'd wanted to be a hands-on boss. Well, now he had that here. In spades.

Job done, he went back to the residence, showered and changed and made his way back to do a ward round. There were only four patients and it wasn't an involved process. Returning the charts to the nurses' station, he paused for a moment and then looked at his watch. A second later, he was striding towards the treatment room. Pulling the curtain aside, he poked his head in. Nothing.

'Are you looking for me?'

Jack arched back. 'Darcie...' He blinked a bit. She stood there in pale blue scrubs, her hair twisted up into a topknot, her face scrubbed clean. She looked...wholesome and...gorgeous. He ordered his pulse to slow down. 'I wondered if you needed a hand.'

'All finished.' Darcie gave a guarded smile. 'We've put Jess on the little veranda ward. It's cool and quiet. Hopefully, she'll get some natural sleep.'

'Good.' He gave an approving nod. 'I was just on my way to get some food. Care to join me?'

'I'd kill for a cup of tea.'

Jack snorted. 'You need something more substantial than that, Dr Drummond. Come on.' He put out a hand in an ushering movement. 'Let's raid the hospital kitchen. They're bound to have a few scraps left over from breakfast.'

A short while later they were tucking into the crisp bacon and fluffy scrambled eggs Carole, the hospital's long-time cook, had whipped up.

'More toast, doctors?' Carole called from the servery window. 'I've made plenty.'

'Thanks, Carole. You're a star.' Darcie sent the older woman a warm smile and made to rise to her feet.

'I'll get it.' Jack's hand landed briefly on Darcie's forearm. 'Finish your food.'

Later, as they sat over big mugs of tea, Darcie said, 'I could sleep for a week.'

'Why don't you, then?' Jack saw her eyes were faintly shadowed. 'At least for the rest of today. I gave you the weekend off, if you recall.'

'I promised to look in on Jess later.'

Jack's mouth gave a mocking twist. 'I think I can just about manage that. Go home to bed, Darcie.'

'You mentioned a debrief.'

'That can wait.'

Darcie's heart began hammering. 'I'd…rather get it over with.'

A beat of silence.

OK. Jack drew in a long breath and let it go. It didn't need rocket science to fathom what was going on here. She was feeling guilty about what had happened in the well when, in reality, if there was any fault to be laid it was down to his actions, not her response. That he'd almost kissed her was beside the point. And she was wound up. He could imagine what her heartbeat was doing under the thin cotton of her scrubs.

And he was technically her boss. That point probably mattered to her. Plus they were sharing job space and home space. There was no room for awkwardness. He had to sort things. 'What happened was a pretty normal reaction,' he said evenly. 'Hell, we saved a life!'

She bit her lip. 'I...suppose.'

'It was just a hug, Darcie.'

Did he really believe that? Darcie fought for control of her wildly see-sawing heart. 'I...don't usually act that way with a senior colleague,' she countered, the set of her small chin almost defiant.

'But, then, I'd imagine you're not *usually* practising emergency medicine at the bottom of a stinking well, are you?'

'No.' She managed a small smile that was almost a grimace. He was spinning things to save her feelings. Well, if that's the way he wanted to play it... But he had to know she'd clung to him and he'd responded by holding her more tightly. He *had* to know that.

But it was his call. For now.

Jack laced his hands around his tea mug. 'If we'd won the lottery and I'd gathered you up in a hug, you wouldn't have thought it odd, would you?'

Her breath caught and fire flooded her cheeks. But they hadn't won the lottery and it hadn't been *that* kind of hug.

And they both knew it.

She couldn't answer. Instead, she lifted a shoulder in a shrug. Jack Cassidy could make of it what he liked.

Darcie slept well into the afternoon. When she woke, she checked her phone for messages and found one from Maggie. She promptly called back.

'Hi, Maggie. What's up?'

'Can you come to my place for a barbecue this evening?'

'Um, yes, I probably could. Something special going on?'

'I wish I knew.' Maggie forced an off-key laugh. 'I've invited Sam Gibson.'

'The new vet in town,' Darcie said.

'I think I must be sick in the head to have started any of this.'

Darcie rearranged her pillows and made herself comfortable. Maggie was usually very much in charge but now she sounded rattled. 'So, what's with you and Sam?'

'He's come round for coffee a couple of times.'

'How did you meet?'

'We had to take our Staffy for his shot. It kind of went from there. He took the boys trail-bike riding yesterday so I thought I should ask him for a meal. A barbecue sounded, well, more casual, I suppose. Only I feel a bit weird just inviting Sam.'

Darcie chuckled. 'You want me there as a buffer?'

'I want you there as a friend! I'm so out of practice with this relationship stuff, Darc.'

'Oh, rubbish! You just need to chill out and enjoy this new friendship that's come your way. Flirt a bit.'

'Flirt!' Maggie squawked. 'How does one flirt again? Remind me. I vaguely remember something about fluttering eyelashes. If I did that, I'd look demented.'

'For heaven's sake, relax and go with the flow. If Sam asks you out on a date, accept nicely.'

'So says the woman who makes a career of not dating *anyone*.'

'I have so been on dates,' Darcie defended.

'Oh, when was that? I'll bet it was so long ago you can't even remember who you went out with.'

'I went out with one of the flying doctors only recently.'

'Brad Kitto?' Maggie dismissed. 'Fly in, fly out. Nice guy but he's a Canadian on a three months' exchange. How was that ever going to amount to anything?'

'OK, OK.' Darcie shrugged off a feeling of discomfort. She didn't need an inquiry into her dating habits, even from someone as well meaning as Maggie. 'But could I remind you this began as a discussion about your love life, not mine.'

'Point taken. So, will you come?'

'Of course...' Darcie gave an exaggerated sigh of acceptance.

'Oh, and invite the big guy.'

'Jack?' Darcie felt her mouth dry.

'Might be a nice chance for him to mix a bit with the locals. And I haven't met him yet.'

Darcie swallowed. She only hoped she and Jack could revert to being at ease with one another. Perhaps going out among a few friendly folk would help. That's if he agreed to it, of course. 'Well, I'll ask,' she said carefully, 'but he's quite likely pretty tired. We had a call-out at five this morning and he's been over at the hospital all day.'

'Mmm, I heard about the emergency from Karen Bayliss. By the way, I've invited her and Zach.'

'Oh, good. They're a nice couple. Would you like me to make a cake for dessert?'

'Oh, would you, Darce? I've spent most of the day trying to get my hair to look less like the ends of a straw broom.'

Darcie's soft laugh rippled. Maggie's colourful take on things always lightened her spirits. 'Shall I come round about five, then? Help you set up?'

'Thanks. And ask Jack,' Maggie reinforced, before she ended the call.

Jack was offhand when Darcie relayed Maggie's invitation.

'Sure. What time?'

'I'm going about five.'

Jack's mouth drew in as if he was considering his options.

'Is that too early for you?' Darcie's gaze was a little uncertain.

'Maybe a bit. Give me the address,' he added, his shoulder half-turned as if he was about to walk away. 'I'll follow on later.'

Information imparted, Darcie watched as he walked out of the kitchen as though he couldn't leave fast enough. As though he was distancing himself from her. Or from the situation they'd found themselves in. That was more likely, she decided.

Swiping up the scattering of flour from her baking, she gave an impatient little tut. This unease was her fault. Why couldn't she have been cool about everything? Laughed it off as the adrenaline rush after having saved a life?

Because she couldn't.

Jack went back to his bedroom. He hated this… distance between them. And he didn't really feel like socialising. God, he just wanted sleep. But he had to show his face. Part of the job. Get to know the locals.

Ignoring what were probably house rules, he flung himself down on the patchwork quilt, boots and all, and stared at the ceiling.

Darcie Drummond.

She'd got to him. He snorted a self-derisive laugh. Perhaps he should just kiss her and get it out of his system. Get *her* out of his system. Yeah, like that was going to help. It would just muddy the atmosphere even further.

He pressed his fingers across his eyelids. He needed to lighten up.

It was early evening when Jack arrived at Maggie's place. The buzz of conversation interspersed with laughter and the mouth-watering smell of steaks cooking drew him along the side path and towards the back garden where he guessed the barbecue was happening.

Maggie saw him the moment he poked his head around the lattice screen. *Wow! Now, there was serious talent.* She smiled and went forward to greet him. 'Jack?' She rolled her eyes in a wry gesture. 'Of course you must be. I'm Maggie. Come and meet everyone.'

Maggie introduced Jack to Sam Gibson, who was officiating at the barbecue. 'Welcome to Sunday Creek, Doc.' Sam's handshake was firm. 'I'm new here myself. Animal doctor,' he enlightened with a grin.

'We're bound to cross paths, then.' Jack laughed.

'But not instruments.' The dry irony in Sam's tone made Jack laugh again. It was going to be OK, he thought. He looked forward to relaxing and enjoying the down time.

'Zach you know, of course.' Maggie was pressing on in her role of hostess. 'And this is Karen, Zach's wife.'

'Hi.' Karen Bayliss gave a friendly little wave. 'And this is our daughter, Molly.' The pride in her voice was unmistakable as she tucked the baby onto her hip.

'How old is she?' Jack ran the tip of his finger along the plump little arm.

'Ten months.'

Jack's mouth crimped at the corners as the little one gave back a haughty look. He felt a twist inside him and the oddest feeling ripped through him. He could have been a father by now if things between him and Zoe had worked out. But for crying out loud! He was thirty-seven. As far as fertility went, he still had oceans of time to find the right woman to have a child with. He shook his head, wondering where the mad rush of introspection had come from.

'She's giving you *the look*,' Karen said with a chuckle.

'She's a princess,' Jack murmured. 'You're very lucky, Karen.'

'Yes, we know.' Karen sent a soft look at her husband. 'We'd almost given up hope when this one trotted into our lives. That's why we chose the name Molly. It means *longed-for* child.'

Out of nowhere, Jack felt drenched in emotion. Hell's bells. He blinked a bit, seizing the escape route with relief when Maggie said, 'And these are my sons, Josh and Ethan.'

'Hey, guys.' Jack shook hands with the two. 'I saw the trail bikes as I came through the carport. You ride a bit?'

'Yep,' Josh, the elder, said. 'Sam took us over to some tracks yesterday. It was awesome.'

'I like skateboarding best,' Ethan chimed in, sensing an interested audience in Jack.

'I used to do that when I was about your age,' Jack said. 'Do you have a bowl here?'

Ethan looked blank.

'Duh.' His brother dug him in the ribs. 'A skate bowl?'

Ethan coloured. 'I just use the concrete paths at the park. But some of the kids use the footpath outside the shops.'

'And you know you're not allowed to do that,' his mother intervened. 'It's illegal.'

'Yeah, I know, Mum.' Ethan gave Maggie a long-suffering look.

'Always good to obey the rules, champ.' Jack grinned, giving support to Maggie's parental role.

'Thanks,' she said, as the boys turned and went off about their own business. 'They're a challenge.'

'They seem like great kids, Maggie. Uh…' Jack raised an eyebrow in query. 'I've brought wine. Where can I stash it? Fridge?'

'Oh, yes.' For the first time Maggie noticed the carry bag he'd parked on the outdoor table. 'Sorry for rabbiting on. Just go up onto the deck. Kitchen's straight through. Darcie's there. She'll organise it for you.'

Head bent, Darcie was busy at the countertop. She looked up, flustered when Jack walked in. 'Hi…' It was no more than a breath of sound.

He gave a tight smile. 'I brought some wine.' He hoisted the carry bag onto the bench. 'Maggie said you'd find a home for it.'

'Oh—OK.' Just looking at him caused a well

of emotion to rise in her chest and lodge in her throat.

He was wearing faded jeans and a simple white polo shirt that showed the tanned strength of his upper arms. The arms that had held her with such caring. Such…tenderness.

She took in a breath that almost hurt and her gaze dropped to his mouth. Desire leached through her. The image of her leaning across the counter to kiss him sent her heart dancing a wild flutter in her chest. A jagged breath snatched at her throat. She didn't do this. Lust after men. And Jack was not some random male. He was a senior colleague. Her boss. She swallowed dryly. 'I'll find some space in the fridge.'

Jack's gaze stayed riveted to her. She was like a sprite in her black sleeveless top and long skirt that dipped round her ankles. He felt like jumping the counter that separated them, whirling her into a mad dance. And then slowly closing in on her so that their bodies were separated only by a whisper of air. And finally…

Darcie closed the fridge and turned back to

face him. She gave him a smile that was gone before it could take shape. 'Have you met everyone?'

'Mmm, think so. Not too many faces to remember.'

'That's always a help.' She picked up a flat-bladed knife to finish off the frosting on her cake. 'Um, would you like a drink? Maggie left instructions for everyone to help themselves.'

'Thanks. I'll get something later.'

Jack propped himself against the countertop, leaning slightly towards her and catching the drift of her light-as-air shampoo for his trouble. 'Cake looks good.'

Tipping her head back, Darcie smiled. 'My contribution towards dessert. I once shared a flat with a pastry chef.' Darcie set the finished cake aside. 'She gave me a few tips along the way.'

'So chocolate cake is your signature dish?'

'It is.' She scooped out a tiny drizzle of frosting with the tip of her finger and pushed the bowl towards him, her gesture inviting him to help her lick the bowl.

He gave a huff of laughter. 'I haven't done this since I was about six.'

'Some catching up to do, then,' she suggested, and he chuckled.

'So, I guess you did this with your mother?' Jack asked.

She gave an off-key laugh. 'My mother doesn't cook. We had a housekeeper. I spent lots of time in the kitchen with her. My parents are history professors. Away on the lecturing circuit a lot. They missed most of my significant milestones when I was at school,' she added as a kind of resigned afterthought.

And wasn't that a crappy way to spend your childhood. 'Were you an only child?' Jack asked evenly.

'Mmm-hmm.' She dragged in a breath and let it out in a whoosh. 'Don't feel sorry for me, Jack.'

'Sorry for you is the last thing I feel,' he countered gruffly.

Their eyes locked and her tongue flicked a tiny dab of frosting from her bottom lip. Jack's throat closed uncomfortably. And for just a moment, a blink of time, there was a connection of shared awareness. Sharp. Intense.

'Hey, you two!' Maggie called, and suddenly their eye contact retracted as quickly as turning off a light switch.

CHAPTER SIX

MONDAY MORNING AND already the barbecue felt like a lifetime ago.

'Thanks for your input, Darcie.' Jack relaxed back in his chair, legs stretched out under his desk. They'd officially completed handover.

'If that's it, I'll do a ward round.' Darcie half rose.

'Hang on a minute.' He flicked a hand in a delaying motion. 'I've arranged for the theatre to be thoroughly cleaned and made sterile. I'm aware it's small but everything's there. If we can keep it ready for emergencies, it will save having to call out the flying doctors, which will in turn save them time and money.'

A beat of silence.

'You're the surgeon and the boss.' Darcie's gaze fluttered down and then up to meet his piercing blue eyes. 'It's obviously your call.'

'But?' Jack's dark brows rose interrogatively.

'We don't have much backup for major trauma.'

Jack all but rolled his eyes. Did she think he was a complete novice at this? He tapped his pen end to end on the desk. 'I'm talking relatively straightforward emergency procedures, Darcie, not heart transplants.'

Stung by his air of arrogance, Darcie said coolly, 'What about anaesthetics? I have a little knowledge but I'm not qualified.'

'I can guide you.'

Well, he obviously thought he had the answer to *everything*. But far from reassuring her, it only added to Darcie's uncertainty. 'I...just don't want us to start playing God every time there's an emergency and think we can automatically sort it here.'

'You don't like me taking over,' Jack interpreted flatly.

Darcie brushed a fingertip between her brows. That wasn't it at all. She wasn't making herself clear. But she'd woken with a headache that morning, her thoughts muddled, her concentration shot to pieces. And all because she couldn't seem to get a grip on her feelings about Jack. She felt very out of her depth but the last thing she needed was her personal feelings spilling over into their professional involvement.

A soft breath gusted from her mouth. Had it been only yesterday they'd been in cahoots like kids, licking frosting from a bowl?

'Didn't you sleep well?' Jack tilted his head, his eyes narrowing. The faint shadows were still there. Her light olive complexion was a dead giveaway.

She lifted her chin. Whether she slept well or not was none of his business.

For a second tension crackled between them, as brittle as spun sugar.

'Could we get back to the point?' Darcie said stiffly. 'I'm more than accepting of your appointment here, Dr Cassidy. The place needs a senior doctor. You're it. Obviously my protocols don't work for you, so change them!'

Jack clicked his tongue. 'It's about trying to get the hospital up and running to its full potential, Darcie. So work with me here, please.'

He scrubbed a hand roughly across his cheek-bones, reminding himself to get some eye drops. His eyes felt as though a ton of shell grit had been dumped there. *He* hadn't slept well. His thoughts had spun endlessly and always centred on this waif of a girl sitting opposite him.

But she wasn't a waif at all. That was just his protectiveness coming into play. And she wouldn't thank him for that. She was capable of taking care of herself. More than. OK. He'd better smarten up. 'Darcie, I need you on board with all these changes, otherwise nothing's going to work for us in any direction, is it?'

His plea came out low and persuasive and Darcie felt relief sweep through her. What he said made sense. They couldn't afford to be offside with one another. Professionally, they were doctors in isolation. It was simply down to her and Jack to make things work. Otherwise she'd have to leave. And she definitely didn't want that.

Where would she go?

'I guess we're both on a bit of a learning curve right now,' she admitted throatily.

'And medically it's been a draining couple of days.' Jack was more than willing to be conciliatory.

Darcie looked at him warily, meshing her teeth against her bottom lip. 'You'll have my support, Jack.'

He let out a long breath. 'Thank you.'

Darcie blinked a bit as he sent her a fence-mending kind of smile. *We'll be OK*, it seemed to imply. Well, she could live with that.

Rolling back his chair, he went to stand with his back against the window. 'The board will be here at eleven for a meeting.'

'Oh—OK.' Darcie rose. She flicked him a wide-eyed query. 'Do you want me there?'

'Silly question.' He paused deliberately, his eyes capturing hers, darkened by the slanting light from the window. 'Of course I *want* you.'

Darcie was still feeling the weight of Jack's parting words knocking against her chest as she finished her ward round.

She'd purposefully left Jessica until last.

'How are you feeling?'

Jess lifted her head from the glossy magazine she'd been reading. 'Much better, thanks.'

Darcie smiled. 'I can see that.' Jess was sitting in the easy chair beside her bed. The hospital gown was gone and she was dressed in a very cute pair of hot pink pyjamas.

'Are you going to release me, Dr Drummond?'

'Let's see what Dr Cassidy has to say, shall we?' Darcie plucked the chart from the end of the bed. She read Jack's notes swiftly. After an initial dose early yesterday afternoon, Jess had needed no further pain relief. Her neuro responses were normal and she'd slept well without a sedative. 'You've bounced back remarkably well, Jess.' Darcie replaced the chart. 'I guess I'm going to have to let you go.'

'Now?' Grinning, Jess threw her magazine aside. 'Cool.'

'Got time for a quick chat first?' Darcie propped herself on the edge of the bed. 'You're quite sure you don't want to go back to your job?'

'Quite sure.' Jess gave a small grimace. 'Too late anyway. I've already resigned and had a friend collect my stuff and bring it in.'

'No problem with contracts and things?'

'It was open-ended,' Jess explained. 'A get-out clause for both parties. They could get rid of me or vice versa.'

'It doesn't sound very secure.'

Jess flapped a hand. 'That's the business I'm in. It doesn't worry me.'

I must be getting old, then, Darcie decided. Because it would worry me. A lot. 'So, what are your plans?'

'Maggie checked to see if there were any flights out of Sunday Creek today. Apparently, one of the local graziers is flying his own plane to a conference in Brisbane this afternoon. He's kindly offered me a seat. I'll go and visit Lachy at the Royal. Then I'll head home to Sydney and start looking for a new job. There are a couple of films happening soon. I'll shoot my CV out. I'll be offered something,' she added with youthful confidence.

'So—obviously, you weren't happy with the film company at Pelican Springs?'

'They took short cuts with safety.' Jess was unequivocal. 'That doesn't work for me.'

Darcie looked thoughtful. So Jack had been right. But, of course, to make charges stick, you had to have people to back up your convictions. And if those same people needed their jobs…?

'I'm OK to go, then?'

Her patient's slightly anxious query jolted Darcie back to her role as Jessica's doctor. 'Just a couple of loose ends to tie up. I'll give you a note for your GP in Sydney and a script for some antibiotics just to be on the safe side. You'll probably be able to have the stitches out in a week or so. And I'll give you a leaflet explaining what's necessary for the care of your wound. This will be an essential part of its healing,' Darcie emphasised. 'Don't neglect it, Jess, all right?'

'I won't,' Jessica promised. 'Mum'll be on my case anyway. But that's what mums do, isn't it?' she added with a philosophical little shrug of her shoulders.

'Yes, I suppose they do.' Darcie's eyes were faintly wistful. She blew out a controlled breath.

'Now, I'll leave your paperwork at the nurses' station. See Maggie before you go. And, Jess, good luck with everything.'

'Oh, thanks, Dr Drummond.' Jess got to her feet, obviously keen to gather her things and get going. 'And thanks for looking after me,' she added with a very sweet smile.

'You're welcome and it's Darcie. We went through a lot together, didn't we?'

Jess nodded. 'I was never so pleased to see anyone as I was to see you at the bottom of that well…' The youngster suppressed a shiver. 'But we did good.'

Darcie smiled. 'Well, make sure you keep *doing good* when you leave here.' She went to the door. Pausing, as if a thought had just occurred to her, she turned back. 'Just to put your mind at ease, Jess, there should be minimal scarring on your arm. Well, nothing the camera will pick up.'

'I'm not a bit worried.' Happy, back in charge of her life, Jess grinned. 'Dr Cassidy said you did a brilliant job.'

* * *

Sunday morning, two weeks later, Darcie rose earlier than usual but it was obvious Jack had risen earlier still. She found him in the kitchen, his hands wrapped round a mug of tea. 'Morning,' she said, helping herself from the pot he'd made.

'Louise Alderton called last night,' Jack said. 'She invited us out to Willow Bend today. I accepted for both of us. I hope that's all right.'

A dimple appeared briefly as Darcie smiled. 'We're taking the day off, then?'

'We've earned it, don't you agree?'

'Well, you certainly have,' Darcie apportioned fairly. 'You've hardly drawn breath since you arrived.' But she wasn't about to question Jack's motives or his workload. He was the boss. He could do what he liked. 'A day out at Willow Bend sounds wonderful,' she said instead. 'What time do they want us?'

'As soon as we'd like. Max will yard a couple of horses for us. Fancy a ride with me?' His gaze lifted, straying momentarily to the sweet curve of her mouth.

'Should be fun,' she said lightly, but if she'd looked in the mirror at that moment she would have seen her flushed image reflecting a wide-eyed vulnerability.

They left for Willow Bend just after nine. As they drove, Darcie said, 'The colours are really something special out here, aren't they? The landscape seems so pure and clean and everything seems so incredibly *still*. The vastness takes my breath away.'

'You're not alone there,' Jack responded quietly, wondering whether this time away from the hospital confines would allow him to get to know her better. He wanted to. So much. But he couldn't rush her. He knew that as well. Perhaps they were destined never to be more than medical colleagues.

Perhaps today would be the day he'd find out.

'I've saddled the horses for you,' Max Alderton said. 'I hope you'll be happy with Hot Shot, Jack. He's fairly spirited.' They were sitting on the homestead veranda in comfortable wicker chairs, enjoying the morning tea Louise had prepared.

'Can't wait.' Jack's look was keen. 'Although it's been a while since I actually did any riding.'

'Hot Shot is a former racehorse,' Louise joined in. 'Nice mouth. Let him stretch out on the flats. Darcie will show you the trails we use.'

'I'll be riding Jewel as usual?' Darcie helped herself to a scone topped with jam and cream.

'Of course.' Louise smiled. 'I think she's missed you. You haven't been out for a while.'

Darcie lifted a shoulder. 'Busy at the hospital. Not that Jack's a slave-driver or anything.' She looked across at him and her breath caught in her throat. Those blue eyes were far too knowing. And suddenly she was afraid. Afraid of what seemed to be happening between them, and whether she wanted it or not.

After morning tea, Jack and Darcie made their way across to the horses. It was a beautiful day, not too hot, with a slight breeze.

A good day just to be alive, Jack thought a bit later, admiration flickering in his eyes as he watched Darcie swing lightly to her mare's saddle, her Akubra tipped rakishly forward and her hair cascading from under it to her shoulders. 'Where are we aiming for?' he asked, deftly circling his own mount to steady the frisky stallion.

Darcie flicked a hand towards a line of lacy willows. 'Louise and I usually cross the creek and head on up to the plateau. The view's amazing from there.'

They took off at a leisurely pace.

'Enjoying it?' Darcie asked after they'd been riding for a while.

'Fantastic.' Jack couldn't believe the sheer exhilaration he felt.

'Oh, Jack, look!' Darcie pointed to a mob of grey wallabies. Alerted to the presence of humans, the quaint little animals were suddenly all flying legs and tails, almost colliding with each other in their haste to leap away to the safety of the scrub.

'Silly beggars.' Jack laughed. Spurred on by the lightness of his mood, he gathered up the reins. 'Fancy a gallop?'

'You're on!' Darcie gave a whoop of delight and took up the challenge.

In perfect rhythm they took off across the paddock, their horses' hooves churning a wake of green through the tall grasses.

Leaving the flat country behind, they climbed higher and higher, until Darcie signalled she was about to stop and wheeled Jewel to a halt halfway up the slope. Her eyes alight with pleasure, she looked down. 'Isn't that something?' she said softly.

Jack reined in Hot Shot beside her, his gaze following hers to the expanse of the valley below, across the faint shimmer of the creek and beyond to the homestead nestling far away on the natural rise of the land.

'Yes, it is…' He closed his eyes, breathing in the woodsy tang of the morning air, tasting it, almost hearing it.

Watching him, Darcie took a long breath, loath to disturb what she perceived as a very private moment. She felt so in tune with him. So, what had happened? Had some fundamental change taken place within herself? And why suddenly today did *everything* about him seem to call to her? As if to clear her thoughts, she raised her gaze to the eastern rim of the cloudless sky. 'Should we head back now?'

'Uh…OK.' Jack blinked a bit, as if reconnecting with the world around him. 'Perhaps we could stop at the creek, spell the horses for a bit?'

The horses were surefooted, picking their way carefully down the track to the creek. Dismounting, Jack looped the reins around Hot Shot's neck, setting him free to graze.

Somewhat guardedly, Darcie followed his example. 'Are you sure they won't take off and leave us stranded?' she asked.

'Not when they have one another for company.' Bending down to the stream, he scooped up a handful of water and drank it thirstily.

'Is that safe?' Darcie bobbed down beside him, her head very close to his.

Jack scoffed a laugh. 'Of course it's safe, Darcie. It's running water! And see over there…' He pointed to where the creek trickled over some rocks. 'That's watercress. And it's lush and green, a sure sign there's no pollution.'

'If you say so, Dr Cassidy.'

Jack chuckled. 'Go on, try it,' he urged, and watched as she dipped her hand into the water and gingerly tasted it.

'It's quite nice.' She gave qualified approval.

'Quite nice?' Jack imitated her crisp little accent to a T. 'It's beautiful.'

She made a face. 'And you're the ultimate authority, I suppose. Jack—' She broke off, laughing. 'What do you think you're doing?'

'Nothing.' He grinned innocently, in the same instant showering her with a spray of water he'd scooped up from the creek.

Darcie shrieked. 'You are such rubbish!' Recklessly, she showered him back until it was a free-for-all battle between them.

'Enough!' Jack finally called a halt, the last of his ammunition slipping between his fingers in a silver rainbow of trickles.

'I'm drenched,' Darcie wailed, peeling her wet shirt away from the waistband of her jeans. 'And cold.'

'Poor baby.' Jack grinned, quite unabashed. 'Want me to warm you up?' He wasn't waiting for her answer. Instead, he reached out and gently drew her towards him, his intent obvious.

'Jack…?'

'Darcie…? Jack looked down at her. A stiff breeze had whipped up, separating tendrils of her hair from around her face and fluffing them out. She looked so vulnerable. And so desirable.

'Should we be doing this…?' Her voice faded to a whisper.

He made a dismissive sound in his throat. 'I've given up trying to find reasons why we shouldn't.'

Darcie swallowed; her heart tripped. He was bending towards her, the deep blue of his eyes capturing hers with an almost magnetic pull. And the sun felt intoxicatingly warm against her back. There was no urgency in the air.

Just a languid kind of sweetness.

Jack was so close to her now she could see the faint shadow across his jaw, the slight smudges under his eyes. Yet his face reflected a toughness, a strength.

'Sweet…' Jack took her face in his hands, his need materialising in the softest sigh before his mouth found hers. The kiss rolled through his blood and raw need slammed into him like nothing he had ever known. Her lips parted and her own longing seemed to match his, overwhelming him like the heady aroma of some dark heated wine.

Applying a barely-there pressure through his hands, he whispered the tips of his fingers down the sides of her throat, then in a sweep across her breastbone to her shoulders, gathering her in.

Darcie clung to him. And the kiss deepened, turned wrenching and wild. She felt a need inside her, an overwhelming need to be touched like this, held like this.

And *stroked* to the point of ecstasy by this man.

But it wasn't going to go that far. At least, not today. She felt Jack pulling back, breaking the kiss slowly, gently, his lips leaving a shivering sweetness like trails of insubstantial gossamer.

A long beat of silence while they collected themselves.

'Oh, help...' Darcie turned away, sinking onto the ground and pulling her knees up to her chin. 'What was that all about, do you suppose?'

Jack settled beside her. 'Does there have to be a reason?' His voice was muted, slightly gravelly. 'We kissed. It's been waiting to happen almost since we met.'

Darcie inhaled a ragged little breath. 'I suppose...'

'I could say you were irresistible, if that will help.'

In a quick, protective movement, Darcie put her hand to her mouth, feeling his kiss return in a wash of quivering nerve-ends. OK, they'd kissed, she owned. But as a result had they opened another set of problems? And where was any of it leading?

'Hey...' Jack turned her head a fraction, tipping her chin up with a finger. 'Don't tell me you didn't enjoy it, Darcie. Because I won't believe you.'

She breathed in and out, a soft little breath through her slightly parted lips. 'It's not that.'

'What is it, then? Surely you know you can trust me.'

'I know…'

'Well, then…'

As if in a dream, she went with him as he gently lowered them to the grassy bank of the creek.

'Darcie…you're beautiful…' Jack buried his face in her throat, his hand sliding beneath her shirt to roam restlessly along her back and then to her midriff, half circling her ribcage, driving upwards until his thumbs, let free, began stroking the underswell of her breast.

With a passion she hardly knew she possessed, Darcie took the initiative, opening her mouth on his, tasting him all over again. And again.

How long they stayed wrapped in their own world she had no idea, but when he drew back and they moved apart to lie side by side, she could tell the sun had shifted, shedding light on the face of the river gums. Her chest lifted in a long steadying sigh. 'How long have we been here?'

Jack shook his head. He felt poleaxed, set adrift without a lifeline. 'Does it matter?' When she didn't answer, he turned to look at her. 'Are you OK?'

What was OK any more? Darcie wondered, pulling herself into a sitting position.

Jack half rose, leaning back on his elbows and surveying her. He didn't like what he saw. Her shoulders looked tightly held, almost shutting him out. 'Talk to me, Darcie.'

For answer, she plucked off a blade of grass and began shredding it. 'I don't know what to say…'

'About what?'

'This—us.'

Jack wrenched himself forward and sat next to her. He held up his hand as if to study it. 'Well, I'm real and as far as I know you're real. We're without ties and single. So where's the problem?' His dark brows hitched briefly. 'You *are* single, aren't you?'

'Yes!' There was a weight of feeling in her voice.

'So I'll ask again. What's the problem?'

She shook her head.

In the silence that followed, Jack reached across and took her hands, brought them to his mouth and kissed each palm. Then, while his eyes said, *Trust me*, he flattened them on his chest. The action brought Darcie very near the edge. Suddenly, without warning, she felt surrounded by him, his masculine strength and the wild pull he exerted on every one of her senses.

'Darcie…?'

'I was engaged, Jack.' Her voice was fainter than air.

'And?'

She swallowed dryly. 'I ran away and came to Australia.'

'So you broke it off. There's no shame in that. I'm sure you had your reasons.'

She pulled in a slow, painful breath. 'Oh, I did.'

Looping out an arm, he gathered her in. 'Going to tell me?' he pressed gently.

Darcie felt the weight of indecision weigh heavily. But if ever there was a time for honesty between them, then it was now. 'His name was Aaron,' she began slowly. 'He was a doctor where I worked at St Faith's in London. A bit older than I. We seemed well suited. We got along. He looked out for me. When he asked me to marry him, I didn't hesitate.'

'But later you began to second-guess your engagement,' Jack suggested quietly.

'Once he'd put the ring on my finger, he changed. Small ways at first so that I thought I'd been mistaken. But then…his caring turned into…control. Control in all kinds of bizarre ways…like how I wore my hair and make-up. He began choosing my clothes, insisting I wear what he'd bought…and that was just the beginning.'

Jack felt the tiny shudder go through her and swore under his breath. 'He wasn't physically abusive, was he?'

'Oh, no.' She shook her head decisively. 'I'd have been gone in two minutes. But, no…his behaviour was the problem. So…manipulative.'

'You did the right thing to get out.'

'You think so?'

'And fast.' Jack frowned a bit. 'What about your parents? Couldn't you have gone to them?'

She shook her head. 'My relationship with them is a bit complex. Sometimes I feel as though I don't know them at all. And they don't know me,' she added in a kind of quiet resignation.

Jack thought long and hard. Something was eating away at her. Whatever else, they couldn't leave things like this. 'Do you want to talk about it?' he offered. 'It goes without saying anything you tell me will be confidential.'

Darcie felt her mouth dry, her breathing become tight. 'Are you being my doctor here, Jack?'

'No, Darcie.' His voice was soft, intense. 'I'm trying to be your *friend*.' When she didn't respond, he took the initiative. Carefully. 'At what part of your growing up did you begin to feel alienated from your parents?'

'From when I was about twelve,' she faltered, after the longest pause.

'You mentioned a housekeeper so I'm guessing you weren't sent away to school?'

'No, but perhaps it would have been better. At least I'd have had company of my own age. I was lonely a lot of the time.'

Jack heard the pain in her voice and a silent oath lodged in his throat. 'Go on,' he encouraged gently, touching her lightly on the shoulder.

Darcie turned to look at him. It had been a feather touch of reassurance, and why it had the capacity to make her reassured she had no idea. But, unaccountably, it did. Words began to tumble out.

'My parents had reached the peak in their careers. They had invitations to speak all over the UK. In between speaking engagements they'd swoop home and gather me up like I was the most important thing in their lives. But in a few days they'd be gone again.'

'Pretty erratic parenting, then,' he said.

She tried a half-laugh. 'I guess you'd say so. And maybe…' she added, as if the thought had suddenly occurred to her, 'that's why I took

Aaron at face value. He was always there for me. Something my parents hadn't been.'

'So, gravitating towards Aaron was a fairly natural reaction on your part,' Jack said. Cautious.

Darcie released her breath on a shuddering sigh. 'I think I was extremely gullible. So easily duped...'

'Hey, don't beat up on yourself. Foresight is a bit scarce on the ground when you really need it.' Concern showed in his gaze as it locked with hers. 'Did your parents ever get to meet Aaron?'

'Of course. We were engaged, planning a wedding. They liked him. If I'd tried telling them what I suspected about him, they'd have thought I was overreacting.'

'But they know where you are now? And reasons why you left England?'

'Yes.'

It seemed a long time until she continued. 'When I began to realise what my life would be like if I married Aaron, I knew I had to get away. I didn't trust myself to confront him because I knew how persuasive he could be. He'd have tried to talk me round.'

Jack rubbed a hand across his cheekbones. He couldn't bear the thought of her being the brunt of such subtle, despicable behaviour. 'Survival is an instinct,' he said quietly. 'So what did you do to survive?'

'I'd become friends with a doctor who'd come over to St Faith's on an exchange, an Aussie girl. When she left to continue her travels she told me if ever I found myself in Australia to let her know, and if I wanted a job she'd see if there was anything going in her old hospital in Brisbane. I called her and explained my difficulty. Within twenty-four hours I was on a flight. I left a note for Aaron, making sure he wouldn't get it until I was airborne.' She paused and then continued, 'I worked in Brisbane for a couple of months but it wasn't the right fit for me.'

'You were still looking over your shoulder.'

She hesitated. 'Perhaps.'

Jack held her more closely. He could imagine her desperation. *Her fear...*

She turned up her face to his. 'I decided to do

a bit of a job search on line. I saw the Sunday Creek vacancy…'

'And one year later, here you are.'

'Yes.' She took one slow breath and then a deeper one, feeling her lungs fill and stretch. It had been such a relief to tell Jack and have him believe in her.

He searched her face for an endless moment. 'Sometimes you look a bit…*haunted* for want of a better word. Do you worry that cretin will find you?'

'Not so much now. It's been ages and he'd never think I'd do something as bold as this.'

Jack snorted. 'He didn't know you very well, then, did he? You are one gutsy lady.'

'Me?'

His eyes caressed her tenderly. 'Yes, you, Darcie Drummond. Thank you for telling me. For trusting me with your confidence.'

Was what they'd done going to change things between them? Darcie wondered as they rode leisurely back to the homestead. It didn't have to, the sensible part of her reasoned. They could still be professional colleagues. But out of hours—what? Best friends? Friends with chemistry? Lovers? At the thought, butterflies rose and somersaulted in her stomach. Now, *that* was a bridge too far. Should she talk to Jack about how they'd handle things? Or not…?

Not, she decided, but her thoughts kept spinning this way and that.

Back at the stables, they unsaddled the horses and gave them a quick rub-down. 'Thank you for a lovely ride, sweetheart.' Darcie looped her arms around Jewel's neck and held her cheek to the mare's smooth coat.

'Are you talking to me?' Jack's mouth quirked into a crooked grin.

'Perhaps I was,' she said, and saw his eyes darken. 'Indirectly,' she added, and laughingly dodged the handful of chaff he threw at her.

CHAPTER SEVEN

IT WAS A week later when Darcie made her way along the corridor to Jack's office. They hadn't seen much of one another recently.

Jack had been away setting up what he called an outreach clinic. But at least he was at the hospital today and Darcie meant to make the most of it.

She knocked and popped her head in. 'Got a minute?'

'Good morning.' Jack heaved his chair away from the desk and beckoned her in. 'Haven't seen you much this week,' he said, as she took the chair opposite.

'No.' Her smile was quick and gone in a flash. She looked across at him. He looked serious and she wondered for the umpteenth time whether he was regretting their kisses and the shift even for a few hours from professional to personal. Maybe he hadn't thought about it at all.

The possibility left her feeling hollow inside.

'How are preparations for the clinic going?' she asked.

'So far, so good. The board members are enthusiastic and the owners of Warrawee station have offered space we can utilise. And it will be a central point and closer for some of the patients than having to travel in here to the hospital. Would you and Maggie have time to put your heads together and work out the basics of what we'll need for the start-up?'

'Of course.' Darcie looked enthusiastic. 'So— starting from scratch, we should think about furnishings for a treatment room and some kind of reception area? Bed, chairs, desk and so on. We can take patient files and laptop on the day. Maybe the whole area will need a lick of paint. And what about a water cooler, tea-making facilities…?'

'Hang on, Darcie.' Jack injected a note of caution. 'Let's just do the basics until we see whether patient numbers indicate it's viable. And it goes without saying all emergencies will still have to come here to the hospital.'

'I realise that. But I think a less clinical environment should work well for our indigenous folk, at least. Some of the elders in particular still have a fear of actual hospitals.'

'You've really got a handle on Sunday Creek and its people, haven't you?'

Darcie's gaze tangled with his as his gentle words soothed all the lonely places in her heart. Breaking eye contact, she said quietly, 'Everyone here has shown me the kind of respect a doctor can only dream about. And I've felt incredibly welcome.'

Jack rubbed absently at his jaw. 'You've obviously earned every bit of trust people have placed in you.'

Darcie coloured faintly, shrugging away his compliment. 'How often would you visualise running the clinic?'

'Perhaps every couple of weeks.' Jack's mouth turned down. 'Depends if folk warm to the idea.'

Darcie sent him an old-fashioned look. 'Establish it and they will come.'

'Let's hope so.'

'Am I going to get a turn or are you intending to keep it to yourself?'

His mouth puckered briefly. 'You may have a turn, Dr Drummond. Now…' Jack placed his hands palms down on the desk '…what did you want to see me about?'

'I'd like a second opinion about a patient, David Campion, age twenty-seven. He's an artist, lives fairly basically in a shack in the bush, according to Maggie. Rather eccentric, I suppose. He wanders in when life gets a bit beyond him.'

The leather creaked, as Jack leaned back in his chair. 'He's not using us as a hostel, is he?'

'No, I'd say not. He seems genuinely under the weather but I can't get a handle on whatever it is.'

'Drug use?'

'I've never detected any sign.'

Jack steepled his fingers under his chin. 'So, what does he live on—the sale of his paintings?'

'They're exceptional.' Darcie warmed to her subject. 'Wonderful outback images. He had a showing at the library not so long ago. I bought two of his smaller prints. They're on my bedroom wall.'

'Is that so…?' Jack's blue gaze ran across her face and down to where the open neck of her shirt ended in creamy shadow. 'I must look in some time.'

Darcie's heart revved at his cheeky remark. She moistened lips that had suddenly gone dry. Did he mean that? More to the point, did she want him to mean it? She swallowed. Was she brave enough to force the issue now, this minute? Go after what her heart was telling her she wanted, needed?

Jack hadn't missed her startled look, or the way her gaze fluttered down. Then back. He gave himself a mental kick. He shouldn't go around making facetious remarks like the one he'd just made. Look into her bedroom? What the hell had he been thinking of? But the remarks had just…slipped out. *Darcie.* Every time he looked at her, he came alive inside.

Wanting her.

But she was vulnerable.

So he shouldn't rush things.

It took him barely seconds to come to that conclusion.

'We'll talk soon, Darcie…'

Darcie caught her breath. The promise in his words was like a husky whisper over her skin, warming her.

For a second she looked at him like a deer caught in the headlights. She waited until her body regained its centre. Then she nodded. She knew what he meant. No explanations were needed.

Abruptly, Jack pulled his feet back and stood. 'Let's have a look at your patient, then, shall we?'

Jack's examination of David Campion was thorough. He ran his stethoscope over the man's chest and back, his mouth tightening. 'Cough for me now, please, David. And again. You've a few rattles in there. When did you last eat?' Folding his stethoscope, he parked himself on the end of the treatment couch.

'Dunno.' David shrugged his thin shoulders. 'Haven't felt hungry.'

'I'm going to keep you in.' Decisively, Jack

began scribbling on the chart. 'You've a chest infection. We'll try to zap it before it turns nasty. I'd like to run a few tests as well, see if we can turn anything else up. Is that OK with you?'

The man blinked owlishly. 'I guess so.'

'We'll get you settled in the ward shortly, David.' Darcie sent her patient an encouraging smile. 'It was good you came in today.'

'A word, please, Darcie.' Jack clicked his pen shut and slid it into his shirt pocket. He stepped outside the cubicle and pulled the screens closed. 'Ask Maggie to get things rolling for David's admission, would you, please?'

'As soon as he's settled, I'll take the bloods,' Darcie said. 'What are we testing for?'

Jack reeled off what he wanted. 'Oh, add hypothroidism as well.'

Darcie frowned. Under-activity of the thyroid gland. 'That's more common in women, isn't it?'

'Perhaps.' Jack lifted a shoulder. 'But we can't take a gender-based view and not test for it. As a case in point, a couple of years ago at Mercy in Melbourne, they had a young *man* of twenty with breast cancer.'

'I guess it would explain David's continued lethargy to some extent,' she conceded.

'There were other pointers,' Jack expanded as they began to walk along the corridor. 'His heart rate was quite slow, plus his skin was as dry as old bones.'

'That could be because of a less than adequate diet and his iffy living conditions.'

Jack's mouth pleated at the corners. 'Well, we'll see when the bloods come back. Ask the lab to email the results, will you? We'll do a CT scan as well. We're equipped to do that here, aren't we?'

'Yes, but the technician is also the chemist, so I'll have to give her a call to come in.'

'Do that, then, please. Interesting case,' he said, as he handed her the chart and continued on his way.

It was a week before David's test results were back. Jack went to find Darcie and together they went along into his office.

When they were seated, she looked at him expectantly. 'So, was it the thyroid, as you suspected?'

'Mmm. Plus his iron stores are abysmally low. But we can treat him.'

'If we can find him,' Darcie warned. 'As you know, he discharged himself after only a day and went bush again.'

'You don't think he'll be at his shack?'

'Unlikely. He told me he has to get several paintings ready for a gallery in Melbourne a.s.a.p. He's possibly taken his swag and easel and gone somewhere to paint.'

Jack tugged thoughtfully at his bottom lip. 'Then we'd better find him and get him started on some medication. See if Maggie can draw us some kind of mud map for the general location where he might be. Fancy a ramble?'

Darcie looked torn. 'Should we both be away from the hospital?'

'It's quiet and it's not as though we're disappearing for the rest of the day.' He curved her a brief smile. 'I'm the boss and I'll take the flak if there's any. Look on it as doing a house call.

If we can find David promptly, I'm hoping we may be able to persuade him to come back to the hospital with us.'

'That would be so helpful,' Darcie agreed. 'The sooner his condition is treated, the better.'

Jack got to his feet. 'That's why we need him here where we can monitor him and get his dose of thyroxine right.'

'That could be David's place through there.' Darcie pointed ahead to where a timber shack was just visible through the belt of spindly she-oaks. They'd been driving for about thirty minutes and Maggie's map had been spot on.

'Well, let's just hope he's home.' Jack brought the Land Rover to a stop.

Picking their way carefully, they climbed the rickety steps, stepping through a fringe of trailing vine to the landing. Raising his hand, Jack knocked and called out but there was no response and no sound from within. He placed his hand on the doorknob. 'Shall we?'

Darcie looked uncertain. 'Perhaps we're being a bit intrusive, Jack.'

'He could be ill and not able to answer the door.'

Jack's logic held up and Darcie nodded her assent.

The door was stuck hard and it needed extra impetus from Jack's knee to get it open. They stepped into the cool interior, which had light coming in from a glass panel at the rear of the building.

They stood there in complete silence until Darcie breathed, 'Oh, my goodness…'

'Wow,' Jack added, clearly awestruck.

The place was filled with artwork, unframed pictures of varying sizes and subjects, ranging from the simplicity of a handful of wildflowers in a jar to the dramatic wildness of a gathering storm.

Darcie's hand went to her throat. 'He's so talented.'

'Amazingly so.' Jack took a step backwards. 'We're treading on very private space, Darcie. I think we should go.'

They left quietly. Descending the steps, they stood for a moment and looked around.

'It's so still, isn't it?' Darcie sounded awed by the silence.

Jack's mouth folded in. 'Might be if the cicadas shut up for two seconds. But I know what you mean.'

It was the middle of the day, the sun high in the heavens, the feathery foliage of bush wattle trees clumping as far as the eye could see. Jack turned his gaze upwards, following the height of the eucalyptus that towered over a hundred feet into the sky. Then out to where the boulders rose up in uneven humps, their reddish-yellow tints like polished brass in the sun. He exhaled a long breath that turned into a sigh. 'David could be anywhere.'

'What should we do, then?'

'I guess we could try a coo-ee and see if we get any answer.'

Darcie knew he was referring to the Australian bush call. 'Go on, then,' she urged.

Jack needed no encouragement. Cupping his hands around his mouth, he called, 'Coo-ee-ee-ee.' The sound, high-pitched, reverberated and echoed back. And back.

They waited.

Nothing.

'Like to try one with me?' Jack's clear blue gaze suggested a challenge. 'Two of us might make a bit more of an impact.'

'Me?' Darcie wavered for a second. 'I've never...'

'Come on,' Jack encouraged. 'It's easy. Follow me.' She did and made a sound between a squawk and an out-of-tune trumpet.

Jack shook his head in disbelief. 'That wouldn't wake a baby! Let's go again. Ready?'

This time she did much better. 'Now I'm getting the hang of it,' she said, clearly delighted with her progress. 'Shall we try again?'

'Third time lucky?' His mouth quirked. 'Let's go.'

But there was still no answering call. Darcie turned away, disappointed. 'I hope he's not lying injured somewhere, Jack.'

'That's not likely. I'd guess he knows this part of the bush like the back of his hand. If he's heard us, he might simply have chosen not to respond.'

Darcie's gaze followed the myriad little bush tracks that ran off into the distance. 'Should we start looking then?'

'No.' Jack vetoed that idea. 'That's not our brief.'

'But David is ill, Jack. He needs treatment.'

'Yes, he does. I'll leave a note for him and shove it under his door.'

'Stress the urgency for him to come into the hospital, won't you?' Darcie looked concerned.

'Why don't you do it, then?' Jack flipped a spiral notebook and pen from his shirt pocket. 'Since David knows you, he might take more notice. While you're doing that, I'll give Maggie a call and check on things there.' Jack began moving to a spot from where he could get a signal for his mobile.

'Did you get on to Maggie?' Darcie asked when he returned.

'Nothing urgent on.'

'So we'll head back to town, then?'

'I think we could hang around a bit longer. David might show and it'd be a shame if we missed him. Let's give ourselves a break and find a shady spot where we can have our lunch.'

'Lunch? You brought lunch?'

He shrugged. 'I threw a bit of stuff together. It's always a good idea to carry food and water when you set out anywhere in this kind of country. Your vehicle can let you down, you can get lost, have an accident. Any number of unforeseen circumstances can see you stranded and waiting hours for help to come. And you don't venture out *anywhere* without telling someone where you're going.'

Darcie made a tsk. 'I *know* all that, Jack.'

'Just reinforcing the message,' he replied evenly. 'Can't have you getting lax.'

'As if!' she huffed, and set about helping him organise their picnic.

'That looks like a good spot over there.' He pointed towards some dappled shade provided by one of the gum trees. 'Bring the blanket from the back seat, will you, please? I'll just check there are no ants.' After a quick inspection he stated that it was OK.

'I see you've raided the hospital linen,' Darcie said, helping him spread the blanket on the grass.

He sent her a rakish grin. 'Are you going to report me?'

'Report you to *you*? Don't think I'll bother. Think of all the paperwork.'

He chuckled. It was brilliant to see her relaxed, upbeat and…happy. And he vowed to keep it that way. If he could. 'I'll just get the cooler.'

'I feel a bit guilty sitting here having lunch while our patient is missing,' Darcie said.

They'd eaten crusty bread rolls stuffed with cheese and cherry tomatoes and were finishing with coffee, from the flask Carole had thoughtfully provided, and some chocolate biscuits.

'We're just making the best use of our time,' Jack rationalised.

Darcie began gathering up the remains of their picnic. 'How long are we going to wait, Jack?'

'Darcie, it's been barely twenty minutes. Do you want us screaming with indigestion? We're entitled to time off but how often do we get it?'

'Not often…' Darcie made a small face. 'Well, not on a regular basis, I suppose…'

'So all the more reason to take it when the opportunity presents itself. And after all we could be considered working,' he said with a grin. 'We're waiting for a patient. Meanwhile, let's get more comfortable.'

When they'd settled themselves against the broad base of the gum tree, Jack turned to her. Raising his hand, he brushed the backs of his fingers gently across her cheek. 'This is good, isn't it?' he murmured.

'It's good…' Darcie voice faded to nothing. Almost without her noticing, he'd moved closer and gathered her in.

And in a second Darcie felt caught in a bubble. The world faded away and there was just the two of them. Her lips suddenly felt parched and she moistened them, her tongue flicking out to wet them.

Jack followed the darting movement and exhaled a long, slow breath. Leaning into her, he claimed her mouth. He tasted coffee and chocolate and was instantly addicted. A shot of adrenaline buzzed through his system. She opened her mouth on his, inviting him in. But he wanted more. Much more. He wanted to lay her back gently on the blanket. Make love to her here with nothing but the deep, rich smell of the earth and the sighs and sounds of the bush around them. His hand shook as it slid beneath her shirt and smoothed the softness of her skin where her waist curved into her hip.

At last the kiss ended. But not their closeness. Jack lowered his mouth to her throat, his lips on the tiny pulse point that beat frantically beneath her chin.

Darcie felt her throat tighten, fluttering her eyes closed as his fingertips idled, taking their time, delicate, like the finest strands of silk.

'Darcie…open your eyes for me…'

She did, every part of her aware of the heat of his body against hers, of that fathomless blue gaze and of a need as basic as her own. Lifting her hands to the back of his neck, she gusted a tiny sigh. 'I wish we could stay here for ever.'

They looked at each other for a long moment, unmoving until Jack reached out a finger and began to twine a silky lock of her hair around it. His gaze softened over her. 'Our time will come, Darcie.'

But obviously not today, she thought resignedly a second later as his mobile rang.

Jack swore under his breath. 'Whoever invented cellphones should be sectioned.'

'Then what would we rely on?' Half-amused, Darcie drew herself to a sitting position. 'Coo-ee calls?'

'Well, not yours.' He grinned, mock-swiping her with the offending phone and scrambling upright.

Activating the call, Jack said, 'Hi, Maggie, what's up?'

'Max Alderton's been injured. Severe neck wound.'

'What happened?'

'Apparently he was out on his motorbike, mustering. He ran into a single-strand wire placed across the track. Louise said it was put there deliberately.'

Jack whistled. 'What's the damage?'

'Profuse bleeding to the right side of his neck.'

'Can we expect arterial damage?'

'Lou isn't sure. Fortunately, Max had his mobile with him. He was able to alert Louise. She's bringing him straight in. I've told her to keep Max sitting up. But he should go straight to Theatre, Jack.'

'Yes.' *In a perfect world.* Jack was thinking fast. 'What staff do we have, available, Maggie?'

'Well, I can scrub in. And providentially Brad Kitto, one of the flying doctors, has just arrived, returning a patient from chemo in Brisbane. He'll gas for you.'

'He's qualified?'

'Extremely.'

'Good.' Jack felt relief wash through him. 'Ask him to scrub and get himself set up, please, Maggie. We'll cane it back now.'

Jack filled Darcie in on the way back to Sunday Creek.

'Oh, how dreadful for Max! And Louise thinks it was sabotage?'

'Seems so. Max has worked Willow Bend for over twenty years. You'd think he'd know if there were any single-strand fences about the place.'

Darcie shook her head. 'He could have been—'

'Decapitated.' Jack didn't mince words. 'If someone was out to injure him, it's an appalling situation.'

'You'll take him straight to Theatre?'

'Yes. Maggie's on it. And fortunately we have an anaesthetist. A contingent from the flying doctors arrived, returning a chemo patient.'

'Oh, that will be Heather Young. We like to keep her overnight and make sure everything's OK before she travels home.'

'And where's *home*?' Jack was concentrating on his driving, keeping the Land Rover at a swift but steady pace.

'Loganlea. About two hundred Ks out. Her family will be in to collect her tomorrow, I imagine.'

'What's Heather's prognosis?' Jack asked.

'Quite hopeful. But with cancer you never know.'

'Obviously you've been managing her care extremely well,' Jack said. 'I'll read the notes when I get a chance.' He glanced down at his watch. 'Another ten minutes should get us there.'

Darcie suppressed a sigh overlaying her concern for Max. In reality they were never off duty.

Already the enchantment of their magical time away from the hospital seemed light years away.

CHAPTER EIGHT

THEY ARRIVED AT the hospital almost simultaneously with the Aldertons. Max was groggy but
conscious. In no time at all they were all inside.

'Didn't need this…Doc,' he slurred.

'Save your strength, Max,' Jack said gently.
'We'll do the best we can for you.' He whipped
out a stethoscope, listening intently, checking
his patient's breathing. 'Seems OK.'

Tossing the stethoscope aside, he very carefully removed the thick towel from around
Max's throat, examining the wound with a clinical eye. 'Main aorta is intact. You've been very
lucky, mate. Clamps, please, Darcie.'

Darcie handed him the instrument resembling
a cross between a pair of scissors and a pair of
pliers. Systematically, he began a temporary
closure of the wound. 'Would you dress it now,
please?'

Darcie was ready with several thick pads to staunch any residual bleeding. 'He's ready for oxygen.' She looked sharply at Jack. 'What capacity do you want it?'

He made a moue. 'Make it eight litres a minute. We'll see what that tells us.'

Darcie worked automatically, dovetailing with Jack as they carried out the emergency procedures. The probe was in place on Max's finger, allowing them to monitor the degree of oxygen saturation in his blood.

'We'll need a cross-match,' Jack said.

Natalie, who had been called in, said quietly, 'I'll sort that.'

'Thanks, Nat,' Jack acknowledged. He began preparing an IV line. 'How's the wound, Darcie?'

'Some seepage, but it's holding. Oxygen sats ninety per cent.' She gave a rundown of the BP and pulse readings. 'I'll get him some pain relief.'

When Darcie returned with the drugs, she could see Jack wasn't taking any chances. Max had been placed on a heart monitor.

Darcie shot the pethidine and anti-emetic home. 'He should begin stabilising fairly quickly. You should get to Theatre, Jack. Go,' she insisted, when he hesitated. 'I can monitor things here.'

'OK.' Jack ripped off his gloves and tossed them aside. 'And find Louise, Darcie. Give her as much support as you can.'

'Of course.' Darcie tamped down a prickle of annoyance. She'd have done that anyway.

Darcie found Louise standing beside the window in the patients' lounge, looking out as if fixed on a spot in the distance.

'Lou?'

Louise spun round. 'How is he?' she asked without preamble.

'He's stabilised. Natalie's just taken him along to Theatre. Come and sit down,' Darcie urged. 'I've asked Carole to bring us a pot of tea.'

'Ironic, isn't it?' Louise sent a distracted glance around the room. 'I never thought when I organised for this lounge to be refurbished that

I'd be one of the first making use of it. Max will be all right, won't he, Darcie?'

Darcie hesitated. In emergency situations no result was ever guaranteed. 'Jack is a fine surgeon.'

'Thank God we have him here.' Louise's statement was heartfelt. 'Otherwise Max would have had to wait hours for the flying doctor to come and then be transported miles away for surgery. How long will the operation take?'

'We can't know that until Jack assesses the extent of Max's injury. Oh, here's Carole with the tea.'

'I've made a few little sandwiches as well,' Carole said. 'Wasn't sure if you'd managed a bite to eat before Mr Alderton had his accident.'

'That's very kind of you, Carole.' Louise gave a trapped smile. 'Thank you.'

'You're welcome, dear.' Carole went on her way.

Darcie poured the tea. 'How did all this happen? Jack mentioned something about sabotage.'

'Something like this makes my blood run

cold.' Louise shook her head as if in disbelief. 'Max is a generous and fair employer. I can't think why anyone would want to hurt him.'

Darcie frowned. 'So, you think it was someone who worked for you?'

'A couple of young farm labourers. Max caught them stealing petrol. We keep large quantities of fuel for the farm vehicles and machinery. Max gave them a warning and they told him they were sorry and they'd only wanted to top up their ute to go to a dance over at Barclay.'

'And Max believed them?'

'He put it down to them being young and wanting a night out. And they offered to pay for it but Max said he'd let it go this time.' Louise took a nibble of her sandwich. 'Then two days ago he caught them at it again. But this time they were filling drums—obviously to sell. As far as Max was concerned, that was the end of their employment. He sacked them then and there and gave them an hour to be off the property.'

'Oh, lord.' Darcie gave her a wide-eyed look. 'So, they've got back at him in this awful way...'

'Looks like it. They knew his daily routine, knew where he'd be and when. They'd seen it often enough. They obviously set up the wire during the night.'

'That's so calculated. And so frightfully scary. Have you spoken to the police?'

'I've given them what information I had and what I surmised had happened. They'll take it from there. My concern has to be for Max and his recovery.' Louise rubbed a hand across her temple as if staving off a headache. 'You'll have to keep him in, won't you?'

'For a few days at least,' Darcie said. 'And Max will have to put up with his food being puréed for a little while. But as soon as he's able to swallow comfortably and if everything else checks out, he should be as right as rain again.'

Louise blinked rapidly. 'You can't imagine the relief to know you and Jack are in charge of our hospital, Darcie. And to have the theatre up and running. That hasn't happened in years.'

'Well, that was mainly Jack's initiative,' Darcie said fairly.

'But you supported it, surely?'

'Of course.' *Eventually.* 'Jack has far more experience than I do,' Darcie said carefully.

Nodding almost absently, Louise glanced at her watch.

'It'll be a while yet, Lou,' Darcie said gently. 'Would you feel more comfortable over at the residence? I'd come and get you when Max is back from Theatre.'

'No, I'm fine here. But thanks.' Louise managed a small smile, looking around her at the array of up-to-date magazines, the colourful mugs and facilities for making a hot drink. She flicked hand. 'Your little touches, I'd guess. Am I right?'

'Nothing worse than sitting in a dreary hospital lounge, waiting for news of a loved one.' Darcie offloaded the praise with a shrug.

'You feel in tune here in Sunday Creek, don't you.'

It was more a statement than a question. Darcie took a moment to answer. 'Yes, I do,' she said simply. And *safer* than she'd felt in her whole life. 'The outback has touched something deep down inside me.' Her downcast lashes fanned darkly across her cheekbones. 'That must sound a bit…odd.'

'Not odd at all.' Louise's green eyes grew soft. 'It's why most of us continue to live out here, through good times and bad. But don't let me keep you, Darcie.' Louise picked up one of the glossy magazines. 'I'll be fine. And you must have a hundred things to do.'

It was late afternoon. At the nurses' station Darcie began writing up her notes on Emma Tynan. The thirteen-year-old had been admitted the previous night with an asthma attack. Thank heaven she was stabilising, Darcie noted, but not as quickly as she would have hoped. 'You know, Nat,' she said thoughtfully, 'I have a feeling Kristy Tynan is still smoking around her daughter. But as usual Emma is totally loyal and noncommittal.'

Natalie shook her head. 'I sometimes wonder who exactly *is* the mother in that family.'

'Kristy works those awful shifts in the truckers' café,' Darcie said. 'It can't be easy for either of them. Do you know if there's a dad anywhere about?'

'Sorry, can't help you there. Kristy and her daughter landed here a couple of years ago. They live in that block of flats near the bowls club.'

Darcie replaced the file. 'Do you think Emma has to fend for herself, then?'

'Well, she'd certainly be on her own a bit with her mother's shiftwork.'

'Poor little thing.'

Natalie gave a frustrated click. 'I can't understand why Kristy can't just ditch the smokes and be done with them.'

'Some folk find it very difficult,' Darcie came in diplomatically. 'It's simply the drug they cling to when they're constantly under stress.'

'I guess so.' Natalie's sympathy showed. 'I could up the percussion on Emma's back if you think it would help. Just to keep an eye on how she's recovering.'

'Yes, it would, thanks, Nat.'

'Oh, look…thank goodness…' The nurse

exhaled a relieved breath. 'Here come the guys at last.'

Darcie swung round. Although neither she nor Natalie had voiced their thoughts, she knew they'd been waiting for news of Max's surgery for the past hour. 'Oh, Brad's here!' Darcie was smiling.

'I thought you knew.'

Darcie shook her head. 'Jack just said one of the flying doctors was going to gas for him.'

Natalie leaned forward confidentially. 'Brad fancies you.'

'Brad's in love with life,' Darcie dismissed, feeling her nerves tense slightly, her cheeks grow warm, as the doctors crossed to the station.

'Hey, *Dee-Dee*!' Brad almost quickstepped to Darcie's side, flinging his arms around her in a bear hug. 'Good to see you, babe.'

Dee-Dee? Arms folded, Jack's gaze narrowed in speculation. What the hell was that about?

Feeling pink and flustered, Darcie disengaged herself from Brad's arms. 'I didn't realise you were the escort bringing Heather back to us.'

'You bet. I had to bribe someone to get the gig.' Brad's white smile flashed briefly. 'Couldn't miss the chance of seeing you. Harry's here too.'

Darcie nodded. 'I saw Harry earlier.' Harry Liston was one of the regular pilots for the flying doctors. 'Are you on turn-around or can you stay with us tonight?'

'Counting on it.' Brad did an impressive little drumroll with his fingers on the countertop. 'Let's have a party, huh? We've brought seafood. Maybe we could gas up the barbecue?'

'Maybe...' Darcie gave a breathless little laugh.

'Natalie, you in?' Brad turned teasing blue eyes on the RN.

'Sorry, I'll have to pass.' Natalie propped her chin on her upturned hand and looked on amusedly. 'I'll be sharing dinner with my two-year-old.'

'That's too bad—'

'Where's Louise?' Jack cut in, his voice trip-wire-tight.

Darcie blinked uncertainly. 'She's here, in the lounge.'

'Wouldn't she have been more comfortable over at the residence?'

Darcie's chin came up. He'd said it brusquely enough to sound like a reprimand. 'I offered,' she replied coolly. 'Louise preferred to wait here. I gather Max's surgery went well?'

'Brad will fill you in. I need to speak with Louise,' he muttered, before striding off.

Watching his retreating back, Darcie fancied she was dodging the invisible bullets he'd fired. But dropping innuendos was not Jack's style. If he had an issue with anyone or anything, he was upfront about it. So what was suddenly bugging him? She turned to Brad for enlightenment. 'There wasn't a problem in surgery, was there?'

Brad pursed his lips as if reluctant to get into it. 'Bit of a glitch when we were halfway through. But we were on it. Max will be just fine,' he confirmed.

Darcie couldn't help the relief she felt, both for Max and Louise but for Jack as well.

A beat of silence, until Brad continued quietly, 'It seems today's surgery was something of a litmus test for the viability of the OR.' He saw her tight little nod and added, 'Jack knows what he's doing, Dee. Trust me. I know a good surgeon when I see one.'

Jack swore silently and darkly as he headed towards the hospital lounge. Did Darcie have something going with Kitto?

Was she sleeping with him?'

He tried the shattering thought on for size. Did it fit?

He hissed a rebuttal through tight lips. That seemed inconceivable. Only a few hours ago *they'd* been as close as any two people could be without actually making love.

Something in Jack's heart scrunched tight.

Surely she wasn't playing him…

Pausing outside the door of the lounge, he took a deep breath, knocked and went in. It took a herculean effort to force his lips into a smile. But his eyes were unable to hide the mixed emotions that stalked him.

* * *

Deep in thought, Jack almost collided with Darcie as they made their way from opposite ends of the corridor some time later. He pulled up short. 'What are you still doing here?'

Darcie all but rolled her eyes. What did he think she was doing there? 'Maggie has to get off. We were just ensuring cover is in place for the night shift.'

'Shouldn't you be over at the residence, looking after our visitors?'

Darcie took a calming breath. There was that innuendo again. She had to be professional here. It was obvious *he* wasn't capable of it. 'They're well able to look after themselves. Lauren's there anyway and I imagine a few more folk will turn up if a party's in the offing. You look like you could do with an evening off yourself.'

Two frown lines jumped into sharp relief between his eyes. 'I need to be here to keep an eye on Max post-op.'

'If you're needed, you're two minutes away at the house.'

'It's fine.' His mouth drew in. 'I'd like to stick around for Louise as well.'

Darcie took a step back as if to regain her space. This was getting too petty for words. 'Why are you being like this?'

Jack folded his arms, leaning back against the wall, challenge like a gathering storm sending his eyes to darkest blue. 'Like what?'

She raised a shoulder uncertainly. 'So…cross.'

'Cross?' The storm broke into harmless little showers and he looked amused.

Darcie sucked in her breath. 'You know what I mean. You're offside with me and with Brad as well. Surely, you should be thanking him for stepping up today.'

'We've debriefed,' Jack said shortly. 'I have no problem with Brad's medical skills.'

Darcie's thoughts were churning but this conversation was going nowhere. 'Lou will want to stay in town tonight. We're a bit full up at the residence…'

'She's made arrangements to stay at the motel. She knows the managers. They'll make her comfortable. In any event, she'll want to stay here with Max for a while longer.'

'Then what?' Darcie pressed determinedly.

'You'll come home and share a meal with the rest of us?'

In other words, pretend to be sociable? Pretend he was oblivious? 'No offence, Darcie, but as the senior doctor I should be here. Today's circumstances were…unusual to put it mildly. But we coped.'

But at what cost? Darcie wondered. Already there was an air of tension emanating from him. Her mouth thinned. If he'd allow her, she could massage his stress away in a second. But the way he was acting around her, he'd probably prefer a one-way conversation with Capone than let *her* anywhere near him. Instead, she held her head high and said clearly, so there would be no mistake, 'Since you've elected to remain on duty, I'll be here first thing in the morning to check on Max. Feel free to catch up on some sleep.'

Jack completed a final ward round and found nothing untoward with any of the patients. Max's status was stable and he'd been placed in the hospital's only private room. Ursula Cabot was a competent night sister so why wasn't he over at the residence, partying with the rest of the team?

Because he was being plain stubborn, wallowing in a pool of self-induced jealousy.

Jack passed sentence on himself, ploughing a hand through his hair in frustration as he made his way along to the hospital kitchen. Ten minutes later he was half-heartedly forking his way through yesterday's casserole, trying to ignore the tantalising aroma of garlic prawns wafting through the window. The seafood barbecue was obviously in full swing.

'Fool,' he muttered, giving up on the casserole and consigning it to the waste bin. He'd acted like a jerk towards Darcie earlier. But the fact was he'd hated to see her wrapped in another man's arms *Hated it.*

He wandered back to the nurses' station, realising the soft hush of night had crept over the hospital without him even noticing.

Ursula Cabot sat under the subdued lighting at the station, her blonde-grey head bent over a crossword puzzle. She looked up as Jack leaned across the counter.

'Would you like a cup of tea, Ursula?'

'No, thanks.' The senior nurse shook her head. 'I've already had several since I came on duty. And you're wearing out the floorboards, Jack. Go home. Isn't there a party going on at the residence?'

Jack lifted a shoulder indifferently. 'I'm just here to keep an eye on things. Max Alderton had major surgery today.'

'And that's why *I'm* here,' Ursula said dryly. 'I checked Max only five minutes ago and I'll keep monitoring him regularly.' She sent Jack a reproving look over the rims of her smart black-framed glasses. 'There's no need for you to keep hovering, Dr Cassidy. I'll call you if I need you.'

Jack's mouth flattened in a thin smile. 'You're chucking me out.'

'Seems like it. Now, scoot. There's dancing happening, by the sound of it. Go and join the fun. Have a twirl around the floor with Darcie. I'll bet that girl's light on her feet.'

Oh, she was. As light as air. At least, that's how she'd felt in his arms.

Jack's thoughts were spinning as he made his way slowly across to the residence. Would he look in on the party? Perhaps. Perhaps not. As he opened the front gate, Capone stirred from his special place under the steps and came to meet him. 'Hello, boy.' Putting out a hand, Jack rubbed the dog's neck as he pushed in against his legs. Then, seemingly satisfied with the small show of attention, Capone gave a feeble wag of his tail, breaking the contact and wandering back to his hidey-hole.

Jack mounted the steps, hearing the music in the form of Norah Jones's husky voice urging someone to 'come away with me'. He dragged in a shallow breath, his normal good sense shattering by the second. Was Brad Kitto even now urging Darcie to do just that? And would she be tempted?

He didn't want to know.

Instead, he bypassed the rec room, where the

party was happening, and made his way along the hall to his bedroom.

Minutes later, he was lying in bed, arms wishboned behind his head, staring at the ceiling. But all he saw was the hurt puzzlement in Darcie's eyes staring back at him. She hadn't understood his stubbornness earlier. Hell, he hardly understood it himself.

How could he have acted like that? As though he was some kind of martyred soul? Had what happened with Zoe destroyed his trust in women so thoroughly? God, he hoped not. Rolling over, he buried his face in the pillow. He had to try to keep his trust in what he and Darcie shared.

Somehow.

CHAPTER NINE

DARCIE CAME THROUGH the silent house, looking for Jack. She finally located him outside, where the morning's soft rays were illuminating the courtyard. He was sitting at the wooden table, nursing a mug of tea, Capone at his side.

'Morning.' She went briskly down the steps.

Jack looked up and felt something shift in his chest. She was dressed in cotton trousers and a pinstriped shirt that moulded every one of her curves. She was femininity in motion.

'I thought you were going to sleep in.' She pulled out a chair and sat down. It was barely seven.

'I did sleep in. How are things at the hospital?'

'Max was in some pain. Brad upped his meds. Otherwise he'd had a reasonable night.'

Jack sent her a mocking kind of look. 'Has our flyboy gone?'

'He left a while ago.' Darcie kept her cool. 'He and Harry wanted to be on their way. We were up before five.'

We? Jack's mouth tightened. Hearing the inclusive pronoun, his worst fear seemed validated.

'So...' Darcie blinked a bit. He seemed suddenly distant, locked down. 'What are you going to do with your day off?'

'I wasn't aware I was having one,' he growled.

Darcie took a deep breath and threw caution to the winds. 'You're acting like a grumpy teen, Jack. I know you're the boss but you need a change of scene. And I'm quite capable of running things at the hospital. There's fishing tackle in the garage. Go and make use of it. Bunbilla Crossing is a good place to start.'

Jack moved his lips in a mocking little twist. 'So says the girl from England.'

Darcie refused to be drawn. 'Take Capone. You seem to prefer his company to that of the rest of us.' She stood and pushed her chair in. 'And I'll expect some decent-sized river perch for dinner tonight.'

* * *

Darcie inspected Max's wound. 'You're looking good, Max.' She smiled. 'We'll review your swallow in a day or so. But so far everything's textbook.'

Max managed a husky 'Thanks'.

She placed a hand on his forearm and squeezed. 'Lauren will replace your dressing now and Jack will see you first thing tomorrow.' At least, she hoped he would.

Darcie was thoughtful as she made her way back to the station.

'Jack for you.' Maggie held up the landline phone.

Darcie's heart skipped. She put the receiver to her ear. 'Jack?'

'Dinner in fifteen,' he said. 'Can you be here?'

'Just about to clock off.'

'Good. See you in a bit.'

'Wait…' Darcie sensed he was about to hang up. 'Did you catch my fish?'

He snorted. 'Of course I caught your fish. Hurry up.'

A trapped smile edged Jack's mouth as he

put the phone down. She'd been right. He had needed to get away from the hospital, if only for a few hours. The break had re-energised him. He'd swum in the river, baked in the sun for a bit.

And caught her fish.

All things considered, he'd fulfilled all the requirements for a satisfactory day off.

Darcie had guessed what he'd needed and that had to mean something.

He couldn't wait to see her.

Darcie's feet had wings as she made her way across to the residence. A sense of relief washed through her. She'd been afraid she might have overstepped the mark, but it sounded as though Jack had accepted her suggestion without rancour and had taken himself off for the day. There'd been a lightness back in his voice. Suddenly life felt good again.

Making her way across the back deck, she popped her head in the kitchen. 'Hi.'

Jack looked up from preparing the fish. 'Hi, yourself.'

She smiled. 'Can you hold dinner for a few more minutes? I need to jump in the shower.'

He waved her away. 'I won't start cooking until you get here.'

Darcie was in and out of the shower in record time, the sweet sting of anticipation slithering up her spine. Bypassing her usual casual cargos and T-shirt, she pulled on a sundress in a pretty floral print, admitting she wanted to look special for Jack. They needed to reconnect. She knew that instinctively.

Taking a moment to look in the long mirror, she decided she'd do. The top of the dress was held up by shoestring straps, showing off the light tan she'd acquired. And just wearing the dress made her feel cool and feminine—and something else.

Desirable?

She stopped for a moment and took a deep breath. There was so much going on between her and Jack. So many undercurrents. He hadn't spelled anything out. Neither had she.

She scooped her hair away from her neck and let it fall loosely to her shoulders. This evening was to be about relaxing. Not supposition. Closing her bedroom door quietly, she went along the hallway, passing the dining room on the way. Stopping, she peered in. Her hand went to her throat. 'Wow…'

'Darcie, you ready?' Jack's voice came from the kitchen.

'I'm here.' She stepped through the doorway into the kitchen.

Jack's eyes swept her from head to toe.

'We're eating in the dining room, I gather?'

'Well, a portion of it,' he countered with a dry smile. He'd set one end of the long refectory table after finding rather elegant placemats and cutlery in a drawer of the big old-fashioned sideboard and had thought, Why not?

'Can I give you a hand?' Darcie's eyes flicked over him, her gaze almost hungry. By now she knew all his features by heart—the clear blue eyes that spelled honesty, the dark hair, always a bit unruly, springing back from his temples, the strength of his facial features, honed to an almost hawk-like leanness. And his mouth—

the gateway to the fulfilment of all her private dreams…

'You could pour us a glass of wine,' Jack said. 'There's a Riesling in the fridge. I thought it would go well with our fish. And Lauren's left some kind of salad.'

'Oh, that was sweet of her.' Darcie brought out the wine and the salad from the fridge. 'How are you cooking the fish?'

'I'll pan-fry it.' Jack raised a dark brow. And then let it rest in the oven for a minute or two. 'Is that all right with you?'

'Perfectly. I'm sure it'll be wonderful.'

It was.

Jack had prepared the fish into chunky fillets, leaving the skin on. Pan-fried quickly, the flesh was crisp, full of flavour and delicious.

'That's the best meal I've eaten in weeks,' Darcie said, replete.

Jack swirled the last of his wine in his glass. 'What about your seafood last night?'

'It was nice,' Darcie allowed, with a little shrug. 'But this was much more special.'

'In what way?' His dark head at an angle, Jack looked broodingly at her.

She swallowed dryly. Even in the subdued light from the candles they'd lit, she could feel the intensity of his gaze. 'Because you cooked it especially for me.' A beat of silence. 'Didn't you?' She felt her eyes drawn helplessly to his.

'I *needed* to do something for you.' He threw back his head and finished his wine in a gulp. 'After my boorish behaviour recently, I thought you might walk,' he admitted candidly.

'Leave?' Darcie almost squawked. 'Why would I do that? Anyway, I have a contract. So unless you're booting me out, Dr Cassidy, I'm not going anywhere.'

Jack couldn't believe the relief he felt. 'So… when will you be seeing Brad again?'

'I have no idea. But he's extended his time here for a couple of months so I imagine he'll be back and forth a bit.'

'You seemed pretty *cosy* with him.'

'And you couldn't wait to make a snap judgement.' Two spots of colour glazed Darcie's cheeks. She knew where he was going with this and felt like thumping him. 'I don't creep around keeping men on a string. That's not my style at all. And if you know anything about me, Jack, you should *know* that.'

'OK…' Jack held up his hand in acceptance. 'I admit to a streak of jealousy a mile wide. I'm sorry for thinking what I did. Deep down I knew it wasn't like you. I—just couldn't seem to get past the possibility…'

Darcie gave a sharp glance at the sudden tight set of his shoulders. So, someone, somewhere had stuffed up his ability to trust. It didn't take much imagination to know where the blame lay. She pressed forward gently. 'What kind of relationship did you have with your former girlfriend? You gave the impression it was just a mutual parting of the ways. But I have to wonder if it was as simple as that…'

'I don't want to talk about it.'

Darcie *tsked* and gave a little toss of her head. 'So, it's OK to have me spilling the facts of my messed-up love-life but not you. How is that fair, Jack?'

It wasn't fair at all, Jack had to admit. But

he'd been left feeling such a fool and worse. He dragged air in and expelled it. 'You want me to talk about this here? Now?'

'The place doesn't matter.' Her voice was soft, intense. 'The telling does. Begin with her name, Jack. And go from there.'

'Zoe,' he said after the longest pause. 'You already know some of the rest of it.'

'Some but not all,' Darcie said calmly. 'Go on.'

He rubbed a hand across his eyes. 'We met in Sydney through mutual friends. We hit it off. Pretty soon we were a couple. Our lives were busy, different, and that's probably what kept everything fresh.'

'But you had such diverse callings,' Darcie stressed.

'Yes.' Jack eased back in his chair, unaware his eyes had taken on a bleak look. 'Back then, Zoe had stage roles so she was working mostly at night. I worked mostly in the day. At first it didn't seem to matter. We grabbed what time we had. Made the most of it.'

Mostly in bed, Darcie interpreted, and felt a

spasm of dislike for this woman who had obviously led Jack a merry dance and then for whatever reason had dumped their relationship and him along with it.

'Zoe wanted to try her chances for work in England.' Jack picked up the thread of the conversation reluctantly. 'It seemed feasible and obviously I didn't want us to be separated so I applied for an exchange. It took a while to organise and Zoe was over there for three months before I could join her.'

'But surely you kept in touch?'

'Of course, but, looking back now, I see it was mostly at my instigation. Zoe just said she was doing the rounds of the casting agents and I understood how much time and effort that took. Then, almost simultaneously, she landed a film part and my exchange came through. I texted her to let her know I was on my way. Told her what flight I was on.'

And he would have been full of expectation and excitement at the prospect of reuniting with his lover. Darcie's heart ached for him. She felt a moment of doubt. Perhaps she shouldn't have started any of this… She held out her hand to him across the table and he took it, clasped it and looked her squarely in the eyes.

She blinked. 'Stop now, if you want to, Jack. I think I know what happened.'

'I arrived in London a day earlier than scheduled.' Jack went on as though she hadn't spoken. 'I went straight to her flat. Zoe opened the door. It was obvious my arrival was unexpected, to say the least.'

Darcie took a dry swallow and tried gently to fill in the picture he was painting. 'She was there with someone else?'

He gave a hard laugh. 'Well, they weren't in bed but near as dammit. She was in a dressing gown and he was parked against the bedroom door, smoking one of those filthy cheroots. I wanted to smash the place up and him along with it.'

Oh, lord. Darcie took a breath so deep it hurt. 'So, it ended then and there? Did you not… talk?' Yet *she* hadn't, Darcie had to admit. She'd just cut and run…

'At that moment there didn't seem much

point.' Jack gave a hollow laugh. 'But we did meet up some time later. Zoe simply said she'd moved on. That *Simon* was an actor, that he gave her what she needed. What I obviously hadn't been able to.'

Darcie heard the pain in his voice. 'You must have been gutted.'

His jaw worked a bit before he answered. 'I just got on with things. I had to. And I am *over* her.'

But there was still a residue of hurt there, Darcie decided. She ran her tongue over her bottom lip. 'That's probably why you didn't enjoy your time in England as much as you should have.'

'Possibly.'

'If you'd been with me, I could have shown you the most wonderful time, the magical places that make England so special.'

A beat of silence.

'I'm sorry you had to leave your country,' he said softly, his gaze, blue, clear and caressing, locking with hers.

'Don't be. Life happens, as they say.' Her

smile was a little forced as she got to her feet. 'Now, what about a cup of tea?'

Jack felt his throat thicken. The need to hold her and kiss her was so urgent he almost jumped up from the table to make it happen. Instead, he let the avalanche of emotion wash over him. 'Tea sounds good.' His jaw tightened for a moment. 'And, Darcie?'

'Jack?' She turned back.

'Thanks for the talk. And the day off.'

They took their tea and some chocolate mints Darcie found and went outside to the courtyard. 'We seem to make a habit of this,' she said, as they made themselves comfortable.

'It's a good place to relax, listen to the night sounds. Are you used to them yet?'

'Mostly.' Darcie made a small downturn of her mouth. 'But the dingoes' howling at night still scares the life out of me. Thankfully, they don't come too close.'

'They're carnivores, for the most part,' Jack said. 'They hunt smaller animals. They only venture closer to civilisation when they can't find food.'

'So I wouldn't find one waiting for me on the back deck, then?

He chuckled. 'Unlikely. And even if you did, the dingo would be more scared of you than you of it.'

'Well, I hope so.' Darcie didn't sound convinced.

'Darcie, they're native dogs, not wolves,' Jack's eyes crinkled in soft amusement. 'The rangers keep tabs on their whereabouts so stop worrying.'

They lapsed into easy silence until Jack said, 'Would you mind if we talked shop a for a bit?'

Darcie gave a throaty laugh. 'I'd be amazed if we didn't. I've held off so you'd feel you'd had a *real* day off.'

'It was good.' Jack lifted his arms to half-mast and stretched. 'Very good.'

'So, where do you want to start?' Darcie said.

'How's Max's recovery?'

'So far, he's checking out well. Pain-free for

most of today. I told him we'll review his swallow quite soon.'

Jack made a moue of conjecture. 'I'd like to leave it for a bit longer.' He paused and stroked his thumb across the handle of his tea mug. 'Brad filled you in about Max's surgery?'

'Yes, he did,' Darcie said slowly. 'He said it was your skill as a surgeon that got him through.'

'Generous of him.' Jack's mouth tightened. 'It was a joint effort. Brad's an instinctive clinician.'

'That's what makes him such a good fit for the flying doctors.'

'Mmm.' Jack's mouth curled into a noncommittal moue. He didn't want the obvious warmth she felt towards Kitto burning a hole in his skull. So, move on. 'The whole episode relating to Max's surgery got me thinking, though.'

'In what way?'

'We need to re-evaluate what kinds of surgery can be safely carried out here. And I want you to know I'd never have attempted Max's surgery without knowing there was a qualified anaesthetist on board. I'd have had Max flown out. You were right to be cautious about opening the theatre.' He held her gaze steadily. 'On the other hand, I was pretty arrogant about what could be accomplished here.'

Darcie's quick glance was very perceptive. As a proud man, she guessed it had cost him something to have admitted his lapse. 'But there was no harm done, Jack.'

'This time.' He gave a jaded laugh. 'I want you to know I would never put you in any position where you felt medically compromised, Darcie. In other words, only the very basic surgical procedures will be done here in future. And whether or not we decide to do them at all will in turn be a joint decision.'

'That's more than fair. Thank you.' After a moment, she continued. 'But I think we need to get this across to the board. And where Louise is concerned, gently, of course. But she took it as read that Max's surgery would happen here. She was grateful and relieved that he wouldn't have to be flown miles away.'

Jack gave a philosophical shrug. 'Well, I'll

talk to her privately about that. As for the rest of the board, they'll have to be made aware that we call the shots about medical protocols.'

Which was what she'd tried to convey in the first place, Darcie thought. But she didn't bear grudges. She was just infinitely glad that the matter had been settled and that Jack had been the one to call it.

'Sunday Creek hospital is very lucky to have you, Darcie Drummond.'

'Pft!' Darcie dismissed the earnest look in his eyes and said lightly, 'It's a team effort between the doctors and the nurses. The practice only functions because of the efforts of both.'

His lips tweaked to a one-cornered grin. 'Well, that seems that matter dealt with. Any news of David Campion?'

Darcie shook her head. 'I'm still hoping he'll make his own way in to us.'

'If he feels grotty enough, he may,' Jack conceded. 'Let's hope your intuition is right.'

'Oh, it will be.' Darcie's lips turned up prettily. She got to her feet. 'Now, I'm going to do the dishes.'

'I'll help you.' Jack was on his feet as well.

'Uh-uh.' Darcie waved away his offer. 'You got dinner.'

'Oh, let's just leave it. I'll bung it all in the dishwasher later,' Jack declared, moving around the table toward her.

In a second she was in his arms.

'About before…' Darcie's look was contrite, her eyes glistening in the muted light. 'I didn't mean to pry.'

'It's fine,' he answered, meaning it. 'And you know what, Dr Drummond?'

She shook her head.

'You're a very good listener.'

'Oh. But I only—'

He kissed her into silence.

'You have the sexiest lips,' he said gruffly, looking down at her.

'Do I?' Her gaze widened and she saw the heat flare in his.

'You do,' he murmured, just before he claimed her mouth again.

Darcie made a tiny sound like a purr and felt a strange lightness, as if love and desire had rolled into one high-voltage surge, sweeping through her body and out to the tips of her fingers and toes. And with a half-formed decision of whatever would be would be, she curled her body into his, each curve and hollow finding a home, a placement, as though they'd been carved out and had been waiting to be filled.

When he pulled back, she felt empty, bereft. She looked up at him, warm honey flecks of uncertainty chasing through her eyes.

Looking at her, Jack felt all his senses go into free-fall. Was this the moment he asked her to go to bed with him? If not now, then when? He agonised for a few seconds, waiting for the words to form. In the almost dark the night air around them began snapping with cicada clicks and simmering with the sharp scent of lemon tea-trees.

'We could take this inside...' he murmured tautly.

Jack's meaning was clear and Darcie felt the nerves grab in her stomach, her mind zeroing in on the fact that they had the house to themselves and there was no one to disturb them. Whatever they chose to do…

'I want to be with you, Darcie. Let me…' His hands stroked up her arms before he gathered her in again, holding her to him so that she felt the solid imprint of him from thigh to breast.

'Jack…' She drew in breath, feeling his hands on her lower back, tilting her closer still, and the wild sting of anticipation pin-pricked up her spine.

'Just say the word.' His plea was muffled against her hair.

Darcie's arms went round his neck, images she'd dreamt about chasing sensible thoughts away. She longed to tell him what he so wanted to hear. But a little voice in her head told her that once they had taken that step, there was no going back. Nothing between them would be simple again.

And there'd be nowhere to hide if it all went wrong.

Nowhere.

Wordlessly, she stepped away from him, wrapping her arms around her midriff. 'Jack—

there's a thousand reasons why we shouldn't go rushing into things.'

'Who's rushing?' He made a sound of dissension. 'This has been waiting to happen for weeks. You *know* we'd be good together.' His voice was husky with gentle persuasion.

Darcie kept her gaze lowered, unwilling to let him see her fears, her vulnerability.

'You're scared, aren't you?'

She licked suddenly dry lips. 'Can you blame me?'

'No.' Jack thrust back against the lattice wall. 'But I blame that piece of work in England who took away your ability to trust your own judgement. But you have to trust again, Darcie. You have to trust *me*!'

Her heart scrunched tight and she shut her eyes against the surge of desire. This was what she wanted, wasn't it? To be a *real* part of Jack's life. Yet something pulled her back from the edge. 'Just give me a little space, Jack. A little more time.'

'Time for what, Darcie?' Jack's voice was without rancour but he was clearly frustrated.

'To start overthinking things. Imagining worst-case scenarios? Come on...'

'Come on, what?' She spun away when he would have contained her. 'You want instant solutions.' Her heart began beating with an uncomfortable swiftness. 'Well, sorry, Jack. I can't give you any.'

Suddenly the atmosphere between them was thick and uncomfortable.

'We have to work together,' she said without much conviction. 'Day in, day out.'

'So what?' He huffed a jaded laugh. 'Are you saying we can't have a personal life outside the hospital?' He pushed a hand roughly through his hair in irritation.

'I'm not being difficult for the sake of it, Jack.'

He shrugged.

Her eyes searched his face. 'We can't leave things like this.'

'I know.'

'How can we go forward, then?'

'I'll back off,' he said, as if coming to a decision.

'I— Thank you.' She forced the words past the dryness in her throat.

His mouth tightened for a second. An intensity of emotion he'd never felt before gnawed at his insides. God, she was so brave and beautiful. He curled his hands into fists to stop them reaching for her. 'The last thing I want is to be offside with you, Darcie. What can we do to make things right again?'

Her uncertainty wavered and waned. She couldn't doubt his sincerity. And she should remember that this was Jack Cassidy, proud and purposeful. And if it came down to it, she'd trust him with her life.

'I suppose we could kiss and make up,' she said softly.

Jack needed no second invitation. Keeping his hands off her by sheer strength of will, he bent towards her, letting his tongue just touch her lower lip as lightly as he could manage when every cell in his body wanted to devour the sweet mouth that opened for him so enticingly. Slowly, slowly, he drew back. 'Sweet dreams, then…' he murmured, and touched his forehead to hers. 'Just make them all about me, hmm?'

Darcie felt the smile on her skin as he touched his mouth to her throat. 'As long as you reciprocate, hmm?'

'Done.' He leaned forward and placed a quick, precise kiss on her lips. Hell, when the time was right, and they'd be able to make dreams into reality, he'd make her feel so *loved*, she wouldn't be able to see straight for a week.

CHAPTER TEN

WITHIN TWO WEEKS Max had been discharged and was doing well. David Campion had come to the hospital and been treated and was now following a health regime Jack had set out for him.

Life was good, Darcie thought reflectively as she updated Emma Tynan's chart at the nurses' station. And although they hadn't actually spelled it out, she felt as though she and Jack had reached a plateau in their personal relationship.

Everything was possible. And the thought lit her up from inside. She made a reflective moue, bringing her thoughts back to Emma. Was there something more she could be doing for the child's wellbeing? She was such a plucky little thing...

'Excuse me, Darcie...'

'Oh, Carole.' Darcie's head came up and she

smiled. 'Sorry, I didn't see you there. I was away with the fairies.'

'That's all right.' Carole looked apologetic. 'I wondered, while it's a bit quiet, whether I could have a word?'

'Of course you can. Let's pop along to my office, shall we?' Darcie led the way, hoping Carole wasn't ill and needing medical advice.

'I won't beat about the bush,' Carole said in her practical way when they were seated. 'I'd like to give in my notice.'

'Oh...' Darcie looked pained. 'There's nothing wrong, is there? I mean, you're not ill or anything?'

'No, no.' The older woman waved away Darcie's concern. 'My daughter and son-in-law have asked me to go and live with them in Brisbane. Ben's just got one of these fly-in, fly-out jobs and he's away a lot. Nicole's feeling lonely and finding it hard to cope with the two little ones on her own.'

'So you're going to help out?' Darcie surmised.

'Well, I'd like to and I do miss the grandchildren. They're lovely little things.'

'Of course they are.' Darcie's tender heart was touched. 'When would you like to go?'

'Well…as soon as you can replace me. But I won't leave you in the lurch,' Carole hastened to add.

'We'll be sorry to lose you, Carole. But I realise things change and family should always come first if possible.'

'That's what I think too,' Carole said, getting to her feet. 'But I'll miss Sunday Creek and all you folk here at the hospital.'

'We must have a little send-off for you.' Darcie smiled, as they walked back to the station. 'And *we'll* do the cooking.'

'Oh—I never expected…' Carole looked suddenly embarrassed. 'But that'd be lovely, Darcie. Thank you.'

Darcie went straight along to Jack's office. As well as Carole's news, she had something else to tell him. She knocked and popped her head in.

'Hey.' He looked up, sending her a quick smile and beckoning her in.

'You were late home last night,' Darcie said. 'I just wanted to check in and ask how things went.' Yesterday had been the opening of their outreach clinic.

'Word had got out apparently.' He leaned back in his chair and stretched his legs out under the desk. 'We were swamped. Lots of follow-up to do. Thank heavens for Maggie's all-round skills. I couldn't have managed without her.'

'So we'll take her each time, then?'

'For the moment.' He rubbed a hand across his forehead. 'I imagine the other nurses would like a turn as well.'

'And me,' Darcie reminded him.

His gaze slid softly over her. 'Of course you, Dr Drummond. Maggie has a list of what else needs to be done to make the space more patient-friendly at the clinic.'

'Excellent. She's on shortly. I'll have a chat to her when she gets in. By the way, Carole's just told me she's leaving. We'll have to find someone to replace her.'

'Oh, no.' Jack made a face. 'I love Carole's spaghetti and meatballs.'

Darcie sent an eye-roll towards the ceiling. 'And on a lighter note, we had news yesterday the MD's house is finished.'

'Mmm,' Jack said absently. 'I know. Louise left me a set of keys.'

'Well, then.' Darcie's look was expectant. 'You should make a time to move in.'

He lifted a shoulder in a tight shrug. 'I'll think about it.' In fact, he had no real desire to move at all. He was quite happy to be living in the communal residence. The MD's house was meant for a family man, wife, kids, dog, the whole box and dice. He'd rattle around like a lost soul. He couldn't think why a needy family in the town couldn't be offered the place instead of him. But he was sure the board would have none of that.

'Meg McLeish will look after the domestic side of things for you,' Darcie said, 'so you only need to gather up your personal stuff and move in.'

One dark brow lifted. 'Keen to get rid of me, Dr Drummond?'

She flushed. 'Your moving doesn't mean

we can't see something of one another outside work.'

He hadn't thought of that. 'Are you saying it could offer us a few *possibilities*?'

Darcie felt the slow build-up of heat inside her. 'Might.'

'We've unfinished business between us, Darcie,' he reminded her softly. 'Don't we?'

She gave a little restive shake of her head, her mind conjuring up a vivid image his evocative words had produced.

She got to her feet. 'If you need a hand with the move, I'm around.'

Darcie was thoughtful as she made her way back to the nurses' station. She found Maggie settling in for her shift. After the two had exchanged greetings, Maggie said, 'Jack tell you we need to organise a few more amenities for the outreach clinic?'

'Leave that for the moment, please, Maggie. I wanted to talk to you about something else.' Darcie swung onto one of the high stools next to the senior nurse, realising without her even knowing it that a possible solution for Emma and her mother had begun crystallising inside her head. 'Do you know anything about Kristy Tynan's personal situation?'

'I know she's a hard worker,' Maggie said. 'Been here a couple of years. Divorced. No man about the place. Keeps to herself.'

Darcie bit down on her bottom lip. 'I don't mean to be nosy here, Maggie but something's cropped up staff-wise.'

Maggie raised a well-defined dark brow. 'Someone leaving?'

'Carole. Relocating for family reasons.'

'And you're wondering whether Kristy would fit the bill?

'My, you're quick!' Darcie grinned.

Maggie smirked. 'Just ask my boys. But, seriously, I think Kristy would jump at the chance to get out of that truckers' café. The hours she has to work are horrendous.'

Darcie looked at her watch. 'I think I'll go and have a chat to her now. The sooner we can get someone for the job, the sooner Carole can go to her family.'

'Working here would certainly be a nicer environment for Kristy,' Maggie reflected. 'And as we're supposed to be a caring profession, I don't imagine the board would object to Emma tagging along when necessary. And we could quietly work on a quit-smoking campaign for Kristy,' Maggie finished with a sly grin.

'You should be running the country,' Darcie quipped. 'But you've read my mind exactly. I'll see you in a bit.'

At the roadhouse, Darcie looked around and then made her way across to what looked like the dining area.

'Can I help you?' a young man, who was wiping down tables, asked.

'I was hoping to have a word with Kristy Tynan,' Darcie said.

'No worries. I'll give her a shout.'

Moments later, Kristy batted her way through the swing doors that led from the kitchen. Recognising Darcie, her hand went to her throat. 'It's not Emma, is it?'

'No, nothing like that, Kristy. Sorry if I startled you,' Darcie apologised. 'But I've come about a job at the hospital. I thought you might be interested in making a change.'

Kristy wiped her hands down the sides of her striped apron, agitation in her jerky movements. 'I don't understand…'

'Could you spare a few minutes?' Darcie looked around hopefully. 'Somewhere we could have a private chat?'

'I'm due a break.' Kristy pulled off her apron and placed it over the back of a chair. 'Let's go outside. There's a bit of a deck where we can sit.'

Quickly and concisely Darcie explained the nature of the job at the hospital. 'You'd be required to plan a menu but it would be nothing complicated, except now and again a patient might have special dietary needs.'

'Well, I could handle that,' Kristy said, looking almost eager. 'I actually did two years of a chef's apprenticeship in Sydney but then I got married and we moved away and I had Emma…' She paused and chewed her lip. 'You probably know I'm divorced now, Dr Drummond. There's just Emma and me.'

Darcie nodded. 'We could offer you more reasonable hours at the hospital, Kristy. And if Emma needed to come with you, that would be fine.' Darcie smiled. 'You could have your meals together and I believe the school bus stops outside the hospital as well.'

Kristy blinked rapidly. 'It seems too good to be true...'

'It's true,' Darcie said. 'Carole, our present cook, is leaving. We need someone just as capable to replace her. And as soon as possible.'

Kristy's mouth trembled. 'So, would I have to come in for an interview or something...?'

'You've just had it,' Darcie said warmly. 'I'll run everything past the board and you'll need a couple of referees.'

'I can manage that.'

'Good. And if everything checks out, then the job is yours.'

'Oh...' Suddenly Kristy's eyes overflowed and she swiped at them with the backs of her hands. 'You can't know what this will mean to Emma and me, Dr Drummond. And thank you for thinking of me.'

'Folk in Sunday Creek have been very kind to me,' Darcie said earnestly. 'I'm just passing it along.'

Later that afternoon, Jack tracked Darcie down in the treatment room. She was suturing the hand of a local carrier who had received a deep wound when unloading roofing iron at a building site. 'Could I have a word when you're finished here, please, Dr Drummond?'

Darcie turned her head. 'Almost done. I'll come along to your office, all right?'

Jack merely nodded. 'Thanks.'

'So, what's up?' Darcie asked, having sent her patient on his way with a tetanus jab and a script for an antibiotic.

Jack stood up from his desk, his expression a bit sheepish. 'I—uh—thought, if you're not busy, we could go across to the house and take a look.'

Darcie's gaze widened in disbelief. 'You haven't been near the place since you arrived here, have you?'

'Didn't see the need.' He came round from behind his desk and began to usher her out. 'Want to come with me, then?'

She shrugged in compliance. 'I'll just tell Maggie where we'll be. By the way, I think I've found us a new cook. I've approached Kristy Tynan. She's keen and I think she'll do a wonderful job.'

Jack whistled. 'Well done, you. Nice footwork there, Dr Drummond.'

'So you approve?'

'Of course. It'll be an excellent move for the Tynan ladies.'

'It will,' Darcie agreed. 'I'll pass the whole thing along to Louise, and she can sort out Kristy's terms of employment and so on. And Carole can get on her way.'

'Oh, we're here already!' Darcie sent him an encouraging look as they pulled up outside the house. 'They've painted the outside as well.'

'Aw, gee,' Jack deadpanned.

'Stop that. It'll be fine,' Darcie said bracingly. 'Let's go inside and see what they've done.'

Inside, the house smelled of new paint and it was obvious the renovation was complete. They wandered from room to room, peered into the master bedroom with its king-sized bed and en suite bathroom, down the hall to two smaller bedrooms, both with their own en suites, and then on to the living room and kitchen.

'It's obvious Lou has had a hand in the furnishings.' Darcie was enthusiastic. 'It's wonderful, Jack, so clean and bright.'

Jack merely looked unimpressed. 'What am I supposed to do with all this space?'

'Live here, one assumes.'

'I suppose I could offer it to the old woman who lived in a shoe,' he grumbled, and sent Darcie a pained look. 'I won't be expected to *entertain*, will I? Give a drinks party before the mayor's ball or something?'

Darcie gave an inelegant snort. 'Don't be pathetic. And as far as I know, Sunday Creek doesn't have a mayoral ball. And look...' she went forward and opened the pantry cupboard '...Meg's already stocked up for you.'

'I just don't need this,' Jack insisted.

'Well, it comes with the MD's position,' Darcie pointed out. 'The board is just fulfilling its part of your employment contract. You have a certain position in the town, Jack,' she reminded him. 'You don't want to be remembered as the rogue medico who wouldn't live in the doctor's residence.'

Jack dredged up a jaded smile. 'Do you think I could coax Capone across to live with me?'

Darcie sent him a look of resignation. She imagined Jack Cassidy could coax a herd of kangaroos to come and live with him if he chose. Her heart dipped. Even *her*. One day. 'I imagine Capone will probably opt to settle here if you offer him a few treats. Oops, that's me.'

Reaching back, she pulled her phone out of the back pocket of her cargos. 'Oh, hi, Lou,' she said brightly. 'Jack and I are just over at the house. It's lovely— Sorry, what did you say?' As she listened, Darcie began making her way slowly along the hallway and out onto the front veranda.

Hearing her abrupt change of tone, and fear-ing something untoward, Jack followed and waited until she ended the call. 'Darcie?'

She turned from the railings, her expression strained. She licked her lips. 'That was Louise…'

'I gathered that.' Jack went to her. 'Is someone hurt?'

'It's Jewel.' Darcie's throat pinched as she swallowed. 'She's stumbled into some kind of rabbit hole. They've only just found her. Her front leg's shattered. Sam Gibson's on his way…' She stopped and blinked.

'Oh, baby…I'm so sorry.' Jack hooked an arm around her shoulders and felt her shaking. 'Do you want to go out to Willow Bend?'

She nodded. 'Lou thought I might want to…' She bit her lips together to stop them trembling. 'My poor little Jewel.'

'Come on,' Jack said gently. 'I'll take you. Just give me a minute to lock up here and let Maggie know what's happening.'

'Do we have some idea where we have to go when we get there?' Jack asked quietly as they drove.

'Not far from the homestead. Louise said she'll keep a lookout for us,' Darcie answered throatily.

Jack put out a hand, found hers and squeezed.

A shadecloth had been erected over the little mare. Jack pulled to a stop a short distance away. 'Go ahead,' he urged gently. 'I won't be far behind.'

Darcie almost ran to where Max and Sam were standing just outside the shelter. Their body language told her everything she'd feared.

Max looked grim. 'Sad day for us, Darcie.'

Darcie turned to Sam, a tiny ray of hope lingering in her questioning eyes.

The vet shook his head.

'C-could I spend a few minutes with her?' Darcie's mouth trembled out of shape.

'Take as long as you need.' Sam's look was kind. 'And Jewel's not in pain, Darcie,' he stressed. 'I've sedated her.'

The little mare was resting on her side. Darcie knelt next to her. 'I'm here, sweetheart,' she murmured, touching her hand to the horse's neck, feeling the soft coat, the already fading warmth. Jewel's big dark eyes opened and Darcie knew she'd been waiting for her.

She touched the velvet ears, rubbed gently along the white blaze on the mare's forehead, her every action rooted in preserving life, until Sam returned to do what he had to do.

Darcie's goodbye was silent. Instead, she held Jewel's head for a moment before burying her face in her soft, shiny coat.

'Time to go, Darcie…' Max looked drawn.

Unable to speak, Darcie raised a hand in farewell and turned blindly into Jack's waiting arms.

He hurried her towards the Land Rover. Making sure they were belted in, he took off swiftly down the track. If there was a shot, he didn't hear it, and silently thanked Sam for his sensitivity. Darcie didn't need that last wrenching finality.

When they hit the main road back to town, he spoke. 'It hurts like hell, doesn't it?'

'Yes, it does.' Her voice broke. Tears made slow rivulets down her cheeks and she wiped them away with the tips of her fingers. Her thoughts spun and became muddled. It wasn't like her to be so emotional. Perhaps it was just past history and other losses, she thought bleakly.

When they neared Sunday Creek township, she asked, 'Could I come home with you, Jack?'

Jack felt his pulse tick over. 'To the new house?'

'If you wouldn't mind...' She didn't look at him, just stared straight ahead.

Jack placed his hand on her thigh. 'Of course I don't mind. I'll just swing by the residence and grab some whisky. I think we could both use a drink.' He flicked a glance at her and saw a solitary tear fall down her cheek. He tightened his fingers in a gesture of empathy. 'I know how bad it feels when you lose a favourite animal.'

'I...don't usually fall apart like this...' Her voice was low, throaty, the admission sounding as if it was wrenched from deep within her. 'I became so attached to Jewel.' She managed a jagged, self-deprecating laugh. 'Perhaps it was just wanting desperately something to love.'

Sweet God. Jack could feel the fine tremor running through her skin beneath his hand. *'I'm here!* he wanted to yell to the treetops. 'Love *me!*' But of course he couldn't.

Jack took down two whisky tumblers from the wall cupboard. 'I can have this neat,' he said. 'But what about you?'

'Is there any ice?' Darcie sat at the breakfast bar on a high stool.

He opened the freezer door. 'There is. Our Meg's a legend.' He shook out ice cubes from the tray and dropped several into her drink. Picking up the glasses, he joined Darcie at the counter.

'Here's to Jewel,' he said softly.

Darcie managed a small smile. She took a mouthful of her drink and blinked a bit. 'It's probably crazy to get so emotional over an animal, isn't?'

'It's not crazy.' Jack stroked her hand, which was curled into a fist on the countertop. 'Animals are wonderful, with hearts as big as the sky. And they're everlastingly faithful. Something humans could learn from.'

A little while later Darcie felt the liquor begin to warm her insides. The trembling had stopped. 'You really get me, don't you, Jack?'

Jack paused giving weight to his answer. 'I think we get each other.' He looked into her face and saw the honesty there. But he also saw the passion. So, what was she telling him? What was she asking him here?

She lifted her glass and took the last mouthful of her drink. 'I don't want to be anywhere else other than here with you.'

Jack's mouth tightened fractionally. 'Are you sure?'

For answer, she leaned across and pressed her lips against his, asking a silent question. She felt his resistance for a second and then he exhaled a breath and his mouth softened. Then it opened and his tongue stroked against her lips and she sighed as he lifted her off the stool and gathered her in. Her whole body quivered and she pressed herself in against him, snaking her arms around his neck and opening her mouth, surrendering it to his.

Passion like she'd never known flared inside her. She pushed her hands into his hair, wanting more than anything to touch him. All of him. Her hands fell to the buttons on his shirt, pulling at them impatiently, almost desperate to feel his naked skin, absorb his heat and craving to get closer.

Jack was momentarily taken aback. This was a Darcie he didn't know. Yet hadn't he always known this was the woman inside the contained little shell she exhibited to the outside world? He could sense her loss of control but, on the other hand, he didn't want her to regret what they were about to do. Pulling away from her mouth, he kissed her throat, trying to slow their ardour. If they were going to make love, he didn't want it to be a hurried affair, over in seconds. He wanted them to *know* each other in the finest way possible.

'Come with me,' he murmured, taking her hands and bringing them to his mouth, pressing a kiss into each palm. He twitched a Jack-like smile. 'Let's try out my new bed, shall we?'

Jack closed the bedroom door softly and for a long moment they looked at each other.

Darcie couldn't believe this was really happening. Yet she knew she'd wanted him for the longest time. Wanted him as much as her next breath. 'Undress me,' she breathed, a tide of need overcoming her, shocking her in its intensity.

'I want this to be about us, Darcie,' he said with a rich huskiness that rippled along her skin. 'You and me. In the truest sense...'

Darcie gasped, feeling his urgency match her own as he flicked open her shirt, bending to put his mouth to the hollow between her breasts, peeling back the lace of her bra, tracing each tiny exposure of skin with his tongue.

With the last item of their clothing peeled away, Darcie couldn't wait a moment longer to burrow in against him. To hold him and be held in return.

'I can hardly believe you've come to me at

last…' Jack's voice was rough-edged with passion held in check.

The softest smile edged her mouth. 'But you always knew I would, didn't you?' She reached out to carry his hand to her breast, standing full and proud as she straightened back.

'Feel. My heart's going wild.'

Jack's mouth dried. She was…magnificent. And soon they would be as one.

Lovers at last.

Darcie had never been so aware of her own sensuality. Leaning down, she patted the clean sweep of the bed. The invitation was in her eyes, her husky feminine laugh almost daring him.

Jack took her challenge, encircling her wrist and twirling her round so she landed on the bed on her back. In a second he was there beside her. Reaching for her, he gathered her close so that they were looking into each other's eyes, their mouths a breath apart.

'God—' Jack brought his head up sharply. 'I don't have anything with me.'

'I'm covered,' she whispered, dazed with emotion. 'Don't hold back, Jack.'

He didn't.

Darcie let all her emotions come to the surface. Soul-destroying scars from the past fell away and she felt as though she'd crossed to another time zone. Jack's touch was instinctive, seeking responses from her she hadn't known existed, touching her deepest senses, sculpting her body from head to toe.

'Let me now,' she whispered, deep in thrall, aching to discover him. His groan of pleasure pushed them closer to the edge and finally, irrevocably, they were lost in the taste and texture of each other, moving in perfect rhythm, climbing even higher where they met in the wild storm of their shared release, drenched in a million stars.

For a long time after, they stayed entwined. Quiet. Even a little amazed that they were there.

In his bed.

Lovers.

'You're smiling,' Darcie said.

'How do you know?'

She brought her head up from where it was buried against his chest. 'Because I am too.' Lifting a hand, she ran a finger along the shadow already darkening his jaw. And stared into his eyes and let her fingers drift into his hair.

Jack touched a finger to her lips, his gaze devouring her. 'No words?'

'No words,' she echoed, feeling her lips tingle where he'd touched them. She burrowed in against him once more.

'Hungry?' Jack asked after a while.

'Lazy, I think. But perhaps a bit hungry too. You?'

'I wouldn't mind a feed,' he admitted. 'But let's have a shower first.'

Darcie raised her head slightly and blinked. 'Together?'

'Of course together.' Laughing softly, he spanned her waist with his hand. 'I'm not letting you out of my sight.

'I'd rather not go out to eat,' Darcie said when they were dressed again and on their way to the kitchen.

'Me neither.' Jack placed a hand protectively at the back of her neck. Going out would somehow break the spell they were under. And that would come sooner rather than later, he decided realistically. 'Let's see what Meg's left us.'

'Left *you*, you mean.' She sent him an indulgent, half-amused look. 'Meg wouldn't know I'd be here.'

They found bread in the freezer, eggs and cheese in the fridge and a can of peaches in the pantry. 'Enough for a feast,' Jack declared. 'Cheese on toast, peaches for dessert.'

'And lashings of tea,' Darcie requested.

'Of course.' Tilting her face towards him, Jack kissed her gently on the mouth. 'English tea for my English rose.'

Cocooned in happiness, Darcie marvelled, 'I can't believe the phone hasn't rung.'

'I can.' Jack flexed a shoulder and grinned. 'I told Maggie we were not to be disturbed for anything less than a multi-trauma.'

'Oh, Jack…' A flood of colour washed over her cheeks. 'Does she know—about us?'

'She'd talked to Sam.' Jack seemed unfazed. 'Maggie got the picture. She said, and I quote, "I'm so glad Darcie has you, Jack."'

'Oh, heavens.' Darcie pressed a hand to her heart. 'Next thing she'll have us engaged.'

'No, she won't.' His mouth worked for a moment. But he thought the idea had real possibilities for all that.

'Will you take me home now?' Darcie asked, when they'd tidied up after their impromptu dinner.

'I'm coming with you,' Jack said. 'I'll move in here by degrees. When it feels right.'

'Oh…' Darcie felt a funny lump in her throat. She wasn't quite ready to share a bed with him on a permanent basis. And she guessed Jack understood that. *Even though I love him.* The realisation nearly tipped her sideways. She wrestled the startling thought back. Instead, reaching up, she placed her palm against his cheek.

Jack nodded. Message received and understood. Turning his head a fraction, he kissed the soft hollow of her palm. 'Let's go home,' he said, his blue eyes steady. 'It's late and I haven't said goodnight to Capone.'

CHAPTER ELEVEN

A WEEK LATER, Darcie and Maggie were sitting at the nurses' station, batting light conversation around, when the phone rang. Maggie turned aside to answer it. 'Bleep Jack,' she mouthed urgently, and began taking details quickly.

Jack came at speed to the station. 'What's up?'

'Another accident out at that movie site at Pelican Springs,' Maggie relayed. 'A stuntman hanging upside down from a tree. Apparently he's caught and they can't release him. They're in a panic.'

Jack swore pithily. 'Still no nurse on the set?'

'Apparently not.' Maggie spun off her chair. 'Let's grab some trauma packs, guys. You need to be gone.'

There was no use surmising anything, Jack decided grimly as they drove. But a few probable scenarios leapt into dangerous possibilities.

'If our patient has been upside down for any length of time, he's quite likely lapsed into unconsciousness,' Darcie said. 'It's going to be tricky, isn't it?'

Jack snorted. 'That's the understatement of the year. We could have a death on our hands, Darcie. Those bastards are obviously still ignoring normal safety protocols. But this time I'll nail them.'

Darcie felt the tense nature of the situation engulf her. Every crisis they faced out here meant delivering medicine in its rawest form. 'Should we run over what we might find? We're going to have to think on our feet from the moment we land there.'

'I've spoken to Mal Duffy.' Jack's response was clipped. 'The SES are on their way, likewise the ambulance and police. Mal's wearing both hats. He's gone ahead and contacted the folk at Pelican Springs. By sheer good luck, the telephone company is doing some work at the property. The phone techs have been using a cherry picker to connect new wiring to the poles. They're on their way to the accident site as we speak.'

'A cherry picker works like a crane, doesn't it?' Darcie's unease was mirrored in her questioning look.

'Mmm. It'll be mounted on the back of a truck,' Jack explained. 'Usually, the operator stands at the control panel at the side of the truck and directs the crane to wherever it's needed. There's a cage-like platform at the top of the crane, of course,' he added. 'The rescue team will ride up in that.'

And that meant Jack himself would go up, Darcie thought tightly. 'I hate this!' she said with feeling. 'We're doctors—not monkeys!'

That brought a glimmer of a grim smile to his mouth. 'It offends me too, Darcie, that these morons think they can get away with treating their workers with such disrespect. Let alone the people who have to come and rescue them from their folly.'

Darcie bit down on her bottom lip. She could tell, even without looking at him, that Jack was strung tight, focused…almost driven. She only hoped he'd keep a cool head. But, of course, he would. They both would.

Because there was no other choice.

The accident site was in chaos when they got there. Automatically, the doctors donned their high-visibility vests and hard hats. 'Here's Mal,' Darcie said with something like relief. 'Perhaps he can tell us what's going on.'

Jack grunted. 'More than that clown Meadows, by the look of it.' Even as he spoke, the unit manager was screaming at the grips—the unskilled workers on the set—to do *something*.

Mal didn't bother with greetings. Instead, he cut to the chase. 'The flying doctors are within a two-hundred-mile radius. We managed to catch them at Harborough station before they turned round to head back to base. If they cane it, they should be here within the hour.'

'Thanks, Mal.'

'Cherry picker's just arrived,' the policeman said. 'Two of the SES guys will go up with you. While you see what can be done medically, they'll start cutting him away.'

'Do we have a name?' Jack's gut clenched. This was a nightmare.

'Wayne Carmody. Sixtyish.'

'Oh, hell...' Jack shook his head. 'What's he thinking of, doing stunt work at his age?' Well, he already knew the answer. This whole set-up was nothing short of illegal. Understaffed and unsafe. Only people desperate for work would consider risking their lives here. 'Right, I'm ready.' Jack creased his eyes against the sudden glare as he looked up at the skeletal outline of the crane. 'Let's get that contraption moving.'

'I'm coming with you.' Darcie's voice showed quiet determination.

'You're not!' Jack's response was immediate and unequivocal.

'We're a team, Jack,' she reminded him, pushing down her own fears. 'We combine our skills.'

For a fleeting moment they challenged each other and Jack's mouth pulled tight. She was as pale as parchment. But as plucky as all get-out. There was no way she'd be left out of this.

'Just do what I tell you, then,' he stipulated, the edges of his teeth grating.

Darcie felt the nerves in her stomach pitch and fall as they were hoisted upwards. Nausea began gathering at the back of her throat and she almost made a grab for Jack. But she fought back the impulse. Instead, she anchored her panic by breathing deeply and holding onto the metal bars of the cage for dear life.

As they reached their target, Jack took in what they had to deal with. Trauma with a capital T. Poor guy. Wayne Carmody was hopelessly entangled, hanging onto consciousness by a thread, his face and arms almost purple with the pressure from his upside-down position.

The crane's operator directed the platform in as close as it would go. 'Best I can do, Doc,' he called from below.

'Thanks—just keep it steady,' Jack yelled back. 'Wayne,' he addressed the rapidly failing stuntman, 'can you hear me?'

The man's response was a bubble of sound.

'Don't lose it, mate,' Jack said. 'We'll have

you down soon.' He turned to Darcie. 'Let's get a non-rebreathing mask on him. It's the only way we can manage the oxygen flow. His BP has to be off the wall. And getting an IV in nigh impossible.'

'I'll get an aspirin under his tongue.' Darcie steadied her position, delving into the trauma kit. It wasn't the ideal solution but the aspirin would begin lowering the injured man's blood pressure and at least alleviate some of the shock his body was undergoing. 'I think there's a possible femur fracture, Jack.' Her worried eyes took in Wayne's right leg, which was hanging at a very odd angle.

'Maybe not. But his circulation has to be critically impaired. We can't tell what we're dealing with until we get him down.' Jack looked up to where the SES team was vainly trying to separate and cut through the thick ropes. 'Come on, guys!' he exhorted. 'Lean on it! What's keeping you?'

'Doin' our best, Doc.' The hard-breathed reply came back. 'Five more minutes.'

The doctors exchanged a swift, tight look,

both acknowledging that the time for a successful rescue was running out.

Darcie kept her gaze focused on their patient until her eyes burned. If they didn't reverse Wayne's upside-down position in the next couple of minutes…

Fear and anguish pooled in her stomach and froze the sunny afternoon, stretching the moments into a chasm of waiting.

'OK—we're about to cut the last of the ropes!' Chris, from the SES, yelled. 'He's all yours, Doc!'

Jack reached up, the muscles in his throat and around his mouth locked in a grimace as he took the brunt of the injured man's weight.

Darcie pitched in, her slender frame almost doubled as Wayne's body descended heavily and fast into their waiting arms and they were able to guide him down onto the floor of the platform.

There were plenty of hands to help them once they were safely on the ground. 'I want the patient treated as a spinal injury,' Jack said tersely. And God knew what else. 'How's the BP, Darcie?'

'Coming down, one sixty over ninety.'

Jack hissed out a breath. He bent closer to their patient. Wayne was dazed and confused, babbling he couldn't feel his legs. Jack brought his head up. 'Will you do a set of spinal obs, please, Darcie?' he asked. As soon as she'd finished, he asked, 'Anything?'

She shook her head. There had been no feeling or sensation in either leg.

'Right, let's give Hartmann's IV, one litre. Stat, please.'

Darcie complied. Did Jack suspect internal bleeding? If he did, then they were hedging their bets here. It was better and safer to give a fluid expander if there was any doubt.

'Flying doctor's landed,' someone said, waving a phone.

'Almost ready for us, Jack?' Zach Bayliss hovered anxiously. This guy looked very bad. The sooner they got him loaded and away the better.

'Just give us a minute to get some morphine into him, Zach.' Jack brought up the dose. 'I'll come with you for the handover.'

'Right, good.' The paramedic looked relieved. 'Where are the flying docs taking him?'

'The Princess Alexandra in Brisbane.'

'It's the best place for him,' Zach agreed.

Jack nodded, proud of his old teaching hospital. The PA was outstanding. The leaders in immediate post-trauma care. And for Wayne it could mean the difference between life and death, or full or partial paraplegia.

'Darcie.' Jack touched her shoulder briefly. 'Check there are no minor injuries to be dealt with, please. I'll be back as soon as I can.'

Good luck, Wayne. The silent wish came from Darcie's heart as she watched the ambulance move away. She felt a shiver of unease up her backbone. This place was beginning to give her the creeps, the tree where the stuntman had been caught rising like some kind of grotesque giant. No, not a nice place at all, she decided. And the sooner they were shot of it, the better...

* * *

'I take it you've put in a call to Workplace Health and Safety?' Darcie said much later, as they drove back to town.

'And the local MP.' The tension in Jack's face had eased remarkably. 'If Meadows and his cronies haven't had their dodgy operations closed down by tonight, I'll raise hell.'

'Mal and his constables took statements from the film crew,' Darcie said. 'Blake Meadows had the hide to say that time meant money and that he wasn't going to hang about.'

Jack snorted. 'I'll bet that went down well with Mal.'

'He told Meadows that if he ignored a police directive, he'd be arrested,' Darcie said with satisfaction. 'Mal was brilliant.'

'So were you, Dr Drummond.' Jack reached across and found her hand, sliding his fingers through hers. 'I—uh—finished moving into the house this morning.'

'Oh—I hadn't realised…' Silence seemed to hang between them, a great curve of it, until Darcie gave an off-key laugh edged with uncertainty. 'Are you going to have a house-warming, then?'

The sides of his mouth pleated in a dry smile. 'I thought we'd already done that.'

Darcie lowered her gaze, at the same time feeling her skin heat up.

'What about coming for dinner?' Jack increased the pressure on her fingers.

Darcie tried to ignore the sudden leap in her pulse as his thigh brushed against hers. 'I think I can manage that,' she said slowly. 'Shall I bring something towards the meal?'

'Not necessary. Just come prepared to stay, Darcie.' Jack's voice had dropped to a deep huskiness. 'I want to hold you all night.'

The following morning Darcie asked if they could debrief.

Jack's dark brows flicked up. 'About Wayne?' They were sitting side by side at the breakfast bar, their mugs of tea in front of them.

'Have you heard anything?'

'I got on to the surgical registrar a while ago,' Jack said. 'Wayne's still with us.'

'Oh, thank heavens. Was it a fractured NOF?'

'Herniated L one, two and three.'

Lumbar vertebrae prolapse, Darcie interpreted. 'It must have happened in the initial fall when the rigging collapsed and left him hanging. Poor man. He must have been in such agony.'

'He's been put on a Fentanyl protocol IV. It's a strong narcotic so I guess his pain is manageable.'

'What about spinal damage? Do we know?'

'He's had MRI and CT scans. Seems OK. I'll check with the surgeon in charge later today.'

Darcie's eyes went straight to his face and slid away. 'Do you ever wish you were back there in the thick of it again?'

A small silence bled inwards, until Jack lifted his mug and drank the last of his tea. 'No, I don't,' he said. 'Why would I, when I can be here with you?'

'Same here...' She looked past Jack to the open window and beyond it, her eyes soft and dreamy.

Watching her expression, Jack took stock. I

don't *ever* want to be away from her, he thought, unbelieving of the avalanche of emotion that arrowed into him. And recognising with stark reality that what he'd had with Zoe now seemed a pale imitation of what Darcie had brought to his life.

Jack Cassidy had fallen headlong in love. The thought scared him, delighted him, amazed him. 'Why don't we get married?'

Darcie's mouth opened and closed. She blinked rapidly. 'Married?' Her voice was hardly there.

'I love you,' he said for the first time.

She took a shuddery little breath. 'I know...'

'And you love me.' His jaw worked. 'You couldn't be with me the way you are, unless you did.'

'Marriage, though...' she countered inadequately. 'We're from such different backgrounds, different countries...'

'Happens all the time,' he drawled, his tone careful and hard to read. 'Just please don't say we hardly know each other, Darcie.'

'No.' She gave a forced laugh. 'That would

be silly. Marriage is an enormous commitment, though, Jack. Doesn't it scare you?'

'Not at all. We're perfect together and I love everything about you.'

'Oh, Jack…' She shook her head. 'I have so much baggage.'

'No, Darcie. You don't.' He lifted her hand and rubbed the knuckles against his cheek. 'You left it all behind at the creek, when we kissed for the first time.'

But it's still there, she thought silently, and carefully reclaimed her hand. 'I need some time to process all this.'

'In other words, you're going to tie yourself in knots.'

Self-preservation hardened her response. 'Well, I'm sorry I can't see everything in black and white like *you*.'

'You're taking this to extremes, Darcie. Hell! I've asked you marry me, not jump off London Bridge!'

Maybe that would have been easier.

'Why do we even have to talk about marriage?' Sheer panic sharpened her words. 'We're all right the way we are.'

He gave a snort of derision. '*Sometimes* lovers. Would you be happy with that?'

Meaning that he wouldn't. 'I'm just grateful for what we have.'

'But it could be so much more!' Sliding off the stool, he strode to the window and turned back. 'So, what do you need from me, Darcie? Just tell me.'

Her eyes clouded. 'I just need you to give me some more space. And no pressure.' She swallowed thickly. 'I don't want to hurt you, Jack, but I won't be pressured into making a life-changing decision.'

'On the other hand, if you could bring yourself to trust me, we could have something amazing together.'

Or broken hearts for ever if it didn't work. She got to her feet. 'I need your word about this, Jack.'

Jack stared at her for a long moment, his jaw clenched, a tiny muscle jumping. He flicked an open-handed shrug. 'If that's what you want...'

What *did* she want? In a moment of self-doubt she wanted to ditch her scruples and accept Jack's proposal. Make a life with him far from everything that had driven her here. But deep down she knew she couldn't make the leap. Not yet. *Perhaps not ever.* She swallowed the razor-sharp emotion clogging her throat. 'That's what I want.'

Three days later at the nurses' station Maggie asked Darcie if she was OK.

'Fine.' Darcie looked up from the computer. 'Why?'

'You seem a bit...distracted.'

The nerves in Darcie's stomach did a tumble turn. 'You're imagining things, Maggie.'

'I'm not,' Maggie insisted.

Darcie huffed a laugh. 'That carry-on the other day out at the film site would make anyone distracted,' she offered by way of explanation. 'I hate administering medicine on the trot like that.'

'Well, Meadows and his lot have left the district,' Maggie said. 'Packed up and gone apparently. And there's an investigation pending. You and Jack will likely be called as witnesses.'

That's if she was still here in Sunday Creek. Darcie felt her throat tighten. 'I thought you were going with Jack to the outreach clinic today,' she said, changing lanes swiftly.

'I cried off. Ethan's not feeling so well.'

'Oh, poor kid,' Darcie commiserated. 'Would you like me to check him over?'

'Thanks, Darce, but he'll be fine. It's just a tummy upset. I'll pop home at lunchtime and take him some new DVDs. Lauren was keen to get a turn at the clinic so it worked out all right. Hey, great news Jack's organised for an ophthalmologist to take a regular clinic out here, isn't it? Quite a few eye problems among our indigenous folk, from all accounts.'

Darcie felt taken aback. 'He didn't mention any of that to me.'

The two looked at each other awkwardly. And then Maggie took the initiative. 'He's got a lot on his plate. Probably slipped his mind.'

Or perhaps he was just taking her request for

space to extremes. Darcie felt her stomach dive. It was all such a mess.

And it couldn't go on indefinitely.

It was early evening the same day and Jack was sitting on his front veranda. Since Darcie's standoff, he'd felt like throwing things. He'd even considered howling at the moon once or twice but that wouldn't have solved anything.

Why the hell had he mentioned the M word to Darcie? Just because it had seemed a good idea at the time. He hated the panic he'd seen on her face. And knowing he'd been the cause of it made it even worse. Idiot! His heart lurched. He should be renamed *Crass* Cassidy.

He had to talk with her. Keeping this ridiculous *space* between them was crazy. 'What do you think, mate?' Reaching down, he ruffled Capone's rough coat. Capone laid his head on his front paws and gave a feeble wag of his tail, before settling. Jack thought about it for one second. 'I guess that's a yes, then.'

Decision made, he got to his feet swiftly and went inside to locate his car keys. He'd go across to the residence now before he could change his mind. Making sure the house was secure, he pocketed his keys and walked back along the hallway to the front veranda.

About to close the front door, he stopped. Headlights lit up the street and a car stopped outside his house. He muttered a curse. Who wanted him now? Was it one of the board members? If it was, why couldn't they come to the hospital in daylight hours like normal people?

He blew out a resigned breath and waited. It was no use pretending he wasn't home as his silhouette was backlit from the sensor light on the veranda. As he waited, the driver's door opened and a figure got out. He blinked a bit. There were no streetlights but unless his eyes deceived him, it was…Darcie?

'Hi,' she called throatily, as she opened the gate and came up the path.

'I didn't recognise the car.' Jack winced at the mundane greeting.

Darcie reached the steps. 'My car wouldn't start. The guys from the garage lent me this one.'

Jack beckoned her up the steps. 'Any clue what's wrong with your car?'

She shrugged. 'One of the mechanics will sort it.' And why on earth were they talking about dumb cars? The nerves in Darcie's stomach twisted. Already, the tension between them was as sticky as toffee. Her shoulders rose in a steadying breath. She had to do what she'd come to do. 'Could we talk?'

Jack felt relief with the force of a tsunami sweep through him. 'Of course we can talk.' He swallowed the sudden constriction in his throat. 'As a matter of fact, I was almost out the door myself. I was coming to talk to *you*.'

'Oh…'

They looked at each other helplessly, unable to bridge the gap.

'OK if we sit here?' Jack waved her to one of the cane chairs on the veranda. 'Or we can go inside.' *Or I can take you in my arms and hold you.*

She shook her head. 'Here's fine.' She took the chair he offered.

'So…' His mouth tightened for a second before he hooked out a chair and sat. 'What did you want to say to me?'

Darcie ground her lip. 'I have some leave due. I'd like to take it.'

Jack sat back as if he'd been stung. This was *not* what he'd been hoping to hear. In the ensuing silence he scraped a hand across his cheekbones, took a long breath and released it. 'When do you want to go? In other words, do you need to make plans?'

'I've made them.' In fact, she'd spent the last couple of hours online, doing just that.

'OK…' He digested that for a minute. 'So, when?'

'There's a flight out tomorrow. I'd like to be on it.'

'To Brisbane?'

She nodded.

Jack suspected he should leave it there but couldn't. 'Well, that's probably a good call. Being in Brisbane will give you easy access to the coast.'

She met his gaze, startled. 'I'm not going to

the coast.' She swallowed past the lump in her throat. 'I'm flying home.'

'Home?' Jack emphasised, feeling as though his heart had been cut from its moorings and was flailing all over the place. 'To England?'

She gave a tight shrug, wishing she'd used another word. But it was out there now. Front and centre.

'I thought you said Australia was home for you now?' A latent prickle of anger sharpened his response.

'I don't want to start playing semantics, Jack.' Suddenly Darcie felt apart and alone. 'This is something I have to do.'

'Why, Darcie?'

'You know why…' She met his gaze unflinchingly, although inside she was quivering. 'I hate the term but I have to say it. I need *closure.'*

'You're going to see *him*, aren't you?' Jack's eyes burned like polished sapphires. 'What, precisely, is the point of doing that?'

'Because I let him get away with everything! I should have stood my ground! Called Aaron on his despicable behaviour. Instead…' She paused painfully. 'I folded like an empty crisp packet. And bolted.'

'Which is what you should have done. God, Darcie...' Jack shook his head in disbelief. 'The cretin isn't worth the plane fare to England. Do you even know if he's still at the same hospital?'

'He's still there. I checked.'

Suddenly the atmosphere between them was crackling with instability.

Darcie felt the quick rise of desire, watching the play of his muscles under his dark T-shirt as he leant back in his chair and planted his hands on his hips. 'Here's another scenario,' he said. 'If you could delay your departure for a couple of days, I could arrange to come with you.'

Her teeth worried at her bottom lip. She felt guilty for not wanting him to accompany her. But he had to understand this was something she had to do on her own. 'Jack—my travel arrangements are locked in. Besides, the board would hardly approve your leave, would they?'

'The board can mind their own business.'

She gave a fleeting smile. 'The running of the hospital *is* their business, Jack. And, honestly, you don't need to feel responsible for me. I know what I'm doing.'

'Have you considered *he* might talk you into giving him a second chance?' Jack didn't look at her because he couldn't. The question he'd posed was too important. Just spelling it out opened a door on a future—their future—that was suddenly treacherous with deep, dark chasms and the crippling effect of stepping into a minefield.

Agitatedly, Darcie began stroking the edge of the table. Jack watched her hands, fine, delicate with short neat nails; doctor's hands.

'He won't, Jack.'

Jack looked up.

She brought her hands together and locked her fingers.

'Loving you has made me strong.' For a long moment she returned his gaze, her intent never wavering. 'He won't talk me round.'

CHAPTER TWELVE

AND THAT HAD been supposed to reassure him? The question ran endlessly through Jack's head for the umpteenth time as he scrubbed his hands vigorously at the basin. Well, he wasn't reassured. Far from it.

'Which one do you want to do first?' Beside him, Natalie began opening a suture pack. She was referring to the twelve-year-old boys who'd been brought in after crashing into each other while skateboarding. Neither had been wearing protective headgear. Both were bloody with split eyebrows and pale with shock at finding themselves in Casualty.

'Doesn't matter. Either one. Idiot kids,' he growled. 'And why weren't they at school?'

Natalie sent him a long-suffering look. 'It's Saturday, Jack.'

'Oh—is it?' he replied edgily. 'I've lost track.'

But he hadn't lost track of the number of days Darcie had been gone. She'd been gone ten days and each had seem to last longer than the one before it.

'Perhaps I'd better take the kid with the egg on his forehead,' Jack reconsidered.

'Matthew,' Natalie supplied. 'Are you concerned he might be concussed?'

Jack shrugged. 'As far as we know, he didn't pass out but I'd like his neuro obs monitored for a couple of hours just to be on the safe side.'

'Need an extra hand?'

Jack spun round from the basin as if his body had been zapped by a ricocheting bullet. His dark brows snapped together. 'You're back.'

Darcie coloured faintly. He didn't seem very pleased to see her and it wasn't the welcome she'd orchestrated in her mind at all. 'I'm back,' she echoed.

'Good trip?' Jack's gaze narrowed.

'Wonderful.'

She looked fantastic. *Shining.* It was the only word Jack could think of to describe her. And she had a new hairstyle. A spike of resentment startled him. But surely it was justified? He'd been here worrying his guts out about her well-being, when she'd been off, obviously having a fine old time in merry England.

'Darcie, hi!' Diplomatically, Natalie jumped in to fill the yawning gap. 'Welcome back. It's good to see you.'

'And you, Nat. And I have presents for everyone,' Darcie singsonged.

'Oh, my stars!' Natalie's hand went to her heart. 'From London?'

'Of course.' Darcie was smiling.

'That's so cool.'

'Could we get on?' Jack yanked his gloves on. He'd had enough of the small talk.

'What do we have?' Darcie directed her question to Natalie.

'Two youngsters, two split eyebrows, two suturing jobs.'

'I'll do one.' Darcie looked directly at Jack. 'Is that OK?'

'If you have the time.' Jack elbowed his way out of the door.

Natalie looked helplessly after him. 'I don't think Jack's been sleeping very well.'

And that was supposedly her fault? Darcie went to the basin. Suddenly her legs felt like jelly. 'Nat, if you've arranged to assist Jack, go ahead. I'm sure I can manage a few sutures.'

'Oh, OK…' Natalie's voice faltered. 'It's so great to have you back, Darcie.'

'Thanks, Nat…' Darcie blew out a calming breath. She'd been buoyed up by excitement, coming back. Now jet lag was suddenly beginning to catch up with her, leaving her flat. She'd sought to surprise Jack but that had obviously backfired. She gave vent to a sigh. Why was nothing in life ever simple? Drying her hands, she shook out a pair of sterile gloves from their packet and went to find her patient.

Darcie did her usual careful job, nevertheless. Placing four stitches in her young patient's wound didn't take long. She completed his treatment chart and handed him over to his mother with instructions to come back in a week to have the stitches removed.

Oh, boy. She wiggled her fingers stiffly. She

must be more tired than she'd thought. But she was determined to wait for Jack. She looked at her watch. It was already late afternoon. Perhaps a cup of tea would revive her. Decision made, she went along to the hospital kitchen.

It was there Jack found her.

'You look like hell,' he said bluntly.

She brought her chin up. 'Fancy that.'

Jack's mouth crimped around a reluctant smile. He put out a hand towards her. 'Let's get you home.'

Outside the air was clear and sharp. Darcie felt a slight dizziness overtake her, the ground coming up to meet her. 'Oh…'

'You're out on your feet,' he growled, wrapping a supporting arm around her shoulders. 'When did you fly in?'

'Very early this morning,' she said, wondering why her eyelids felt weighted down. 'But then I had to coordinate two flights to get home to Sunday Creek.'

'No wonder your body clock's out of whack. You need sleep.' He stopped at his Land Rover and opened the passenger door. Scooping her up, he lifted her in.

'Did you miss me?' She mumbled the words against his shoulder as he settled in beside her.

'You bet I did.' His gaze softened. 'I should never have let you go without me. Did you miss me?' He turned his head, waiting for her answer, but she was already asleep.

Darcie woke to silence and the gentlest breeze wafting through the partly open window. Blinking uncertainly, she half raised her head. Where was she? She looked around at the unfamiliar prints on the walls, the white linen blinds. And then reality struck. She was in one of the guest bedrooms in Jack's house.

She muffled a groan into the pillow. He must have got her to bed after they'd left the hospital. What else had he done? Cautiously, she put a hand under the duvet and touched the softness of the jersey pants she'd worn on the flight. Except for her shoes, he hadn't attempted to undress her. 'Oh, Jack…' A smile curved gently around her mouth. 'You are such an honour-able man.'

The sharp click of the front door closing had her sitting boldly upright, pulling her knees up to her chin. 'Jack?' Her voice came out throat-ily. 'Is that you?'

'Ah...' Jack's dark head came round the door. 'Sleeping Beauty's awake, I see.'

Darcie blushed, watching him amble into the bedroom, his powerful masculinity making the space appear to shrink to doll's-house propor-tions. 'Good sleep?' he asked.

'It was. Sorry I passed out on you,' she said ruefully. 'What time is it?'

'Five-ish.'

Darcie frowned. 'Five-ish when?'

'Sunday afternoon.'

'You mean I've slept the clock round?'

He looked at her with steady eyes. 'Jet lag will do that to you every time. How about some din-ner? Hungry?'

'Starving.' She smiled a bit uncertainly. 'But at the moment I need the bathroom more than I need food.'

A wry smile nipped his mouth. 'See you in a bit, then. Oh, I swung by the residence and picked up your suitcase.'

'Oh—thanks for that.' She watched as he slipped out and retrieved it from the hallway.

'I've made minestrone.' He hefted her case onto the end of the bed. 'Hurry up.'

Darcie threw herself out of bed and into the en suite. Were they back together? Properly back together? She ground her lip in consternation, letting the rose-scented gel drift silkily over her body and puddle around her feet. They hadn't parted on the best of terms. Jack had clearly not been happy about her reasons for going to England. But surely he wouldn't have brought her here to his home if he was still offside with her?

Air whistled out of her lungs, ending in an explosive little sigh as she dressed quickly. Conjecture was getting her nowhere. She left the bedroom, an odd flutter of shyness assailing her as she made her way along the short length of the hallway to the kitchen.

Jack had set places at the table. Standing for a moment, she watched him, her gaze lingering, drinking in his maleness. He was wearing a black T-shirt that delineated the tight group of muscles beneath and a pair of washed-out jeans. 'Something smells good.'

He turned from the stove, eyeing with obvious approval her sleek black leggings and pearl-grey top. 'Feeling better?'

'Much.' She joined him at the stove. 'Anything I can do to help?'

He turned off the heat and gave the minestrone a final stir. 'Couple of bowls might be a good idea. And there's some multigrain rolls in that bag there. Then we'll be in business.'

'Another?' Jack's look was softly indulgent a little later as Darcie neared the end of her second bowl of soup.

'Heavens, no!' She gave an embarrassed laugh. 'But that was truly delicious, Jack. Thank you.'

His mouth pulled at the corner. 'You're more than welcome, Darcie.' He looked at her guardedly. 'Coffee?'

She shook her head. 'Perhaps later.'

He shifted awkwardly in his chair. 'Sorry for acting like a prat when you arrived yesterday.'

Eyes cast down, she made a little circle with her finger on the tabletop. 'Do you want to hear about my trip?'

Jack's heart was beating like a tom-tom. Lord, how he'd missed her! And now she was back, barely centimetres away from him, her faint, delicate fragrance teasing his senses, making a mockery of his control. 'I suppose we should get it out of the way.' Standing to his feet, he collected their used dishes and took them across to the sink.

Darcie had the feeling of being dismissed. But not for long. She rose from the table, moving purposefully across to join him at the window, peering out. 'The reason I went, Jack, was to come to you whole. If you want us back together, the least you can do is listen.'

Something in Jack's heart scrunched tight. He blinked and turned his head a fraction. Her eyes were cast down, her long gold-tipped lashes fanning across her cheeks. He felt a lump the size of a lemon in his throat as he swallowed.

'You're right. But let's get more comfortable, shall we?'

They went through to the lounge room. Darcie switched on the two table lamps and a gentle glow of light flooded the room. Jack held out his hand and guided her to the big, squishy sofa. Once they were seated, he looped out an arm and gathered her closely. 'OK.' He took a deep breath and let it go. 'Fire away.'

Darcie's heart quickened and she edged back so she could look him in the eye. 'I saw Aaron.'

His jaw tightened for a moment. 'How long did you spend with him?'

'Not long. Needless to say, he was stunned to see me. I didn't bother with small talk. I just hit him with everything. I let him have it all—everything I'd been feeling. How his behaviour had been reprehensible, how he'd sapped my self-worth and a whole lot more.'

Jack's eyes burned with a strange intensity. 'How did he react?'

'He folded. Apologised. Several times, in fact.' Her eyes clouded briefly. 'I suggested he should get some specialist psychiatric help. It's obvious he's deeply unhappy.'

Jack sent her a guarded look. 'How did he respond to that?'

'He said he's already in therapy.' A breath of silence. 'I…said I hoped it worked. Then I got up and left.'

'Were you upset?' Jack asked carefully.

'Maybe a bit. But I felt free. It was a fantastic feeling.'

'My gutsy, brave girl.' Jack pulled her close again. 'I'm so proud of you.'

'Wait until you hear what else I did.'

'Good grief.' Jack shook his head. 'Better hit me with it then.'

'I went to see my parents. They were actually home for once.'

'And?'

'I had a very frank talk with them.' She sent him a dazzling smile. 'On the flight over to England the thought came to me that they hadn't shaped up very well as parents. There was you and your big loving family and you obviously had a happy childhood. Maggie doing so well as a single parent, and Nat with her husband working away so much, managing to keep her little girl safe and happy. And my parents took none of the responsibility that comes with parenthood. They're bright people. They *should* have known.'

Jack blinked and blinked again. Sweet heaven, she was lovely. His gaze slid softly over her. 'So, what was the outcome?'

'For the first time we sat together like a family. And we talked. Really talked.' Darcie's mouth wobbled a bit. 'They both apologised for their lack of involvement but assured me over and over that they'd always loved me. And Mum cried. And Dad called me his *darling girl*.'

Jack's throat constricted. 'You continue to amaze me, Darcie.' He held her more closely, his lips making feathery kisses over her temple. 'So you had your big talk. Then what? Dare I ask?'

'They're coming to our wedding!'

Jack looked at her, startled.

Her breath caught. 'That's if you still want to marry me…?'

'Oh, God, yes!' he said hoarsely. 'With bells on.' In one liquid movement he hauled them both upright. In a second their bodies were surging together like breakers dashing to the shore.

They kissed once, fiercely, possessively. And again. This time slowly, languidly, taking all the time in the world to savour each other. To reconnect.

On a little whimper Darcie burrowed closer, drinking him in, feeling the absorption of his scent in her nostrils, through her skin.

When they drew apart, they stared at one another, the moment almost surreal. 'We're getting married,' Jack said.

'Yes.' She reached up and drew her finger along his throat and into the hollow at its base. 'And I want everything, Jack. A real outback wedding. I want our little bush church decorated with masses of flowers, big bows on the seats and the church filled with family and friends.'

Jack looked bemused. 'And after?'

'We'll hire a marquee and find somewhere

special to put it. And we'll have fairy-lights and maybe a dance floor and glorious food.'

Jack's eyes went wide in alarm. 'I won't have to cook, will I?'

Darcie snickered. 'Of course not. We'll fly caterers out from Brisbane if we have to. And don't look like that,' she chided gently. 'My parents are paying for everything. I bought a wedding dress in London,' she added shyly. 'I hope you'll like me in it.'

'Of course I'll like you in it.' There was a gleam in his blue eyes. 'And out of it too.'

Darcie laughed, feeling the warm flood of desire ripple through her body. 'We just have to make a date, then.'

'Let's leave that for tomorrow. Right now, we need to be doing other things. Don't you agree…?'

'I agree, Jack.' The catch in his voice told her everything she needed to hear. A slow, radiant smile lit her face as she slipped her hands under his T-shirt, loving the smooth sweep of his skin against her palms. Loving *him*. 'Now,' she enticed coyly, 'come and unwrap your present.'

CHAPTER THIRTEEN

IT WAS A perfect day for a wedding.

'Darcie, could you possibly stand still for a half a second?' Maggie did a slow inspection around the now dressed bride. They were at the residence with barely fifteen minutes left before they were to leave for the church.

'I'm so happy I could burst, Maggie.'

'Don't do that,' Maggie pleaded. 'I'd have to fasten these tiny buttons all over again.'

'What do you think of the dress?' Darcie posed in front of the full-length mirror. 'Does it look OK?'

'OK?' Maggie's voice went up an octave. The dress was a stylish combination of silk and hand-made lace with a fitted bodice, tiny cap sleeves and slim-cut skirt. 'Honey, you look stunning.' Maggie's gaze had a misty look. 'Jack's eyes will be out on stalks.'

'That's if he can see at all,' Darcie said dryly. 'I can't believe his brothers hauled him off to the pub for a buck's do the night before the wedding!'

'Well, boys will be boys,' Maggie countered practically. 'And, anyway, Jack stuck to the soft stuff mostly, according to Sam.'

'Mmm.' Darcie didn't seem convinced.

'Oh, Darce.' Maggie laughed. 'Relax, would you? Even if Jack ended up a bit tipsy, he's had all day to sleep it off.'

Darcie gave a reluctant chuckle. 'Then it's lucky we decided to have the wedding in the late afternoon, wasn't it? For everyone's sake.' She paused and sobered. 'Maggie, thank you so much for standing up with me and for your endless kindness and friendship.'

'Oh, tosh.' Maggie shook her dark head. 'Friendship is a two-way street. And yours has been invaluable to me as well. Now, hush up.' She gave an off-key laugh. 'Or we'll both be bawling and ruining our make-up. Shame you're not getting a honeymoon, though.'

'Price of being doctors in the outback.' Darcie

looked philosophical. 'But we're getting a couple of nights away. Jack's arranged for someone to fly us across to the coast. Posh hotel and all the trimmings.'

'Oh, yes...' Maggie waggled her eyebrows. 'Breakfast in bed?'

Darcie's face went pink. 'All that. I'm so happy, Maggie.'

'Sweetie, you deserve it.' Maggie's look turned soft. 'Oh, I meant to ask, how are your parents enjoying Sunday Creek?'

'They're loving it.' Darcie picked up their bouquets of red roses and handed one to Maggie. 'It was so sweet of Louise to invite them to stay at Willow Bend.'

'Willow Bend is such a beautiful property,' Maggie agreed. 'And they'll get a real taste of station life as well.'

'Your transport's here.' Lauren stuck her head in the door. 'Oh, my stars! Darcie, you look incredible!'

'Oh...thanks, Lauren.' Darcie gave a shaky laugh. Suddenly she was all butterflies. What if Jack didn't turn up? What if his brother, Dom, forgot the rings? What if they both messed up their vows? With trembling fingers she reached up to touch the delicate silver heart at her throat. Jack's gift to his bride. She blinked back the sudden possibility of tears. 'Do we have time for a glass of wine?'

'No, we don't,' Maggie said firmly. 'It might be fashionable to be late but personally I think it's plain bad manners. Besides which, Jack will be wearing out the carpet and the priest will be getting tetchy.'

'Oh, he won't,' Darcie remonstrated. 'He's been lovely to us.'

'Come on, guys.' Lauren began to usher them out into the hallway. 'Your chariot awaits.'

'Do you have all our stuff, Lauren?' Maggie raised a quick hand in question.

Lauren held up her big purple holdall. 'Spares of everything and the bride's pashmina in case it gets chilly later.'

'Thanks. You're a star.'

'Happy to be your lady-in-waiting,' Lauren said cheerfully, and the little party began to move forward to the front veranda.

'Wh-what's that?' Darcie's voice squeaked with shock. She pointed to the buggy and two handsome grey horses that were drawn up outside.

'It's your transport,' Maggie said. 'Isn't it fabulous?'

Darcie's mouth opened and closed. 'But Louise promised to lend us their Mercedes!'

'She did.' Maggie grinned. 'And it's for Lauren and me. You, my dear, are travelling in style by horse and coach.'

'You wanted a real outback wedding,' Lauren reminded the bride.

'But horses!' Darcie looked helplessly between the two women.

'Aren't they a picture?' Maggie looked so pleased. 'Sam found them for us. And they're accustomed to this kind of thing, so you'll be quite safe.'

'Besides, the locals will want to wave to you along the way,' Lauren put in. 'You'll be like a princess.'

Darcie began to laugh. 'I can't believe you've all done this to me!'

'Oh, we're not devoid of innovation out here,' Maggie said innocently. 'Now, here's your dad come to escort you.'

'Good afternoon, ladies.' Professor Drummond greeted the little group and then took his daughter's hands, holding her at arm's length, his gaze suspiciously moist. 'Darcie…you look radiant. And so grown-up…'

'Oh, Dad…' Darcie choked back a slight lump in her throat and thought this was how it should be on her wedding day. It would have been unthinkable if her father had not been here.

'You look very lovely, Maggie.' The professor took his eyes off his daughter for a moment.

'Thank you, Richard.' Maggie acknowledged his compliment with a dignified little nod.

'Richard!' Lauren hissed in a shocked stage whisper. 'Isn't that a bit disrespectful? Isn't he a *lord* or something?'

'No.' Maggie snickered behind her hand. 'He asked us to call him Richard when he and Darcie's mum hosted a pre-wedding do a few days ago.'

'Now, are we ready, ladies?' Professor Drummond tucked Darcie's arm through his and pro-ceeded to walk her carefully down the flight of shallow steps.

Darcie aimed her bouquet towards the horses and buggy. 'Are you all right about this, Dad?'

'It's really quite comfortable.' He turned his head and smiled at her. 'And our driver, Jay, is a very interesting chap. We had a most pleas-ant journey in from Willow Bend.'

'You came all that way in a buggy?' Darcie was astounded at her usually conservative fa-ther's easy acceptance of the rather *out-there* mode of transport for her wedding.

'Here, Darcie, give me your flowers while you hop aboard,' Maggie instructed. 'And don't panic. The seat is well sprung and it's spotlessly clean. You'll arrive in perfect order.'

'I'm just grateful I'm not wearing a hooped skirt,' Darcie vented as she placed her foot gin-gerly on the buggy's running board.

'Then we might have had a problem,' Maggie conceded, watching as Darcie settled back in the red leather seat and reclaimed her bouquet.

'Safe journey.' Maggie gave a jaunty finger wave and stepped back. 'See you at the church.'

Darcie's heart was cartwheeling as she stood in the church porch beside her father.

'You look beautiful, darling,' he said. 'Jack is a very lucky man. And a fine one,' he added with obvious approval.

Darcie took a steadying breath. 'Is he here, Dad? Can you see him?'

Maggie, who had arrived seconds earlier, said briskly, 'Of course he's here!' Lifting a hand, she brushed a tiny tendril of hair from Darcie's cheek. 'Now, are we ready?' she whispered.

Darcie nodded and swallowed.

'Good.' Maggie gave a smile of encouragement. 'Then let's do it.'

Standing in front of the altar, Jack felt his chest rise in a long steadying breath. She was here at last, his English bride, his Darcie, his love. She had almost reached him when he turned, lifting a dark brow in admiration.

Seeing the familiar broad sweep of her bridegroom's shoulders, the proud set of his head, Darcie stifled a whirlpool of nerves and found the impetus to walk the last few paces to his side.

'OK?' he murmured, reaching for her hand. Darcie nodded, and clung for dear life.

'Welcome, guys.' Standing in front of them, Father Tom Corelli beamed across at the bride and groom. 'Now, before we get on to the real business, I believe you have something personal you wish to say to each other.'

'Thank you, Father.' Darcie struggled with her prickling eyes and turned to face Jack. He smiled encouragingly at her and they took hands. Darcie drew in a steadying breath and began.

'Jack, you are my rock. You have listened to me and supported me both personally and professionally. My love for you is as wide and deep as the outback sky. You are my true north. And I will love you always and for ever.'

Raw emotion carved Jack's face and he wished he'd thought of something so poetic. But he'd do the best he could.

'Darcie, you are my true love. You are as strong and brave as the finest trees of our forests, yet as tender and beautiful as our most delicate wildflower. And I will love you always and for ever.'

Darcie made the rest of their formal vows in a haze of happiness, hardly registering when she and Jack exchanged rings. When Father Tom pronounced them husband and wife, they kissed. And kissed again to a ripple of applause and a few whistles from one or two daring members of the Cassidy clan.

Smiling broadly, the priest ushered them to an especially prepared table at the side of the altar. And as they sat to sign the register, Lauren delighted them by singing a huskily sweet rendition of 'The First Time Ever I Saw Your Face'.

'I had no idea!' Darcie's whisper was shot with amazement.

'Just our little surprise for you.' Jack's expression was tender. 'And I have another for you as well, Mrs Darcie Cassidy.'

'Oh?' Darcie blinked and tried to speak and

wondered if it was possible to overdose on sheer happiness.

Jack's smile began slowly and then widened. 'We're having a proper honeymoon,' he said. 'A whole week to ourselves. We've got us a locum.'

Darcie looked fascinated. 'Who?'

There was a gleam in Jack's blue eyes. 'One of the flying doctors.'

Darcie's eyes flashed wide in disbelief. 'Are we talking about Brad Kitto here?' she whispered.

Jack nodded. 'As a wedding present, he's kindly offered to give up a week of his leave for us.'

Darcie was dumbfounded. 'But Brad?' she emphasised in a stage whisper. 'You always looked on him as something of a rival.'

'That was then.' Jack seemed unfazed.

'But didn't you feel uncomfortable about accepting his offer?'

'Why would I?' Jack looked at his bride, his entire heart in his gaze. 'After all, my love, you'd chosen *me*.'

* * * * *

April

May

June